"Are those names ringing any bells, Marcus?"

He hated to dash the spark he'd seen in Bethany's eyes, but he shook his head. "None."

Bethany pulled out a photo of his squad. "This was taken two days before the ambush." She sat beside Marcus, pointing out the surviving rangers. She rattled off their names, but all he heard was the beating of his heart as the sweet scent of her hair wafted into his nostrils. Nothing about the ambush or his teammates seemed familiar...but she did.

Bethany glanced up at him and her eyes widened, probably at the spark of attraction Marcus was sure was blanketing his face. The familiar wide blue eyes and graceful curve of her face called to him. He reached out and stroked her jaw, moving downward to her lips. She didn't pull away, at least not at first. Her head bobbed backward and her breathing heightened. He wanted to kiss her, just as he had a hundred times before in his dreams. It was her he'd been remembering. He'd never been more certain of anything in his life.

Virginia Vaughan is a born-and-raised Mississippi girl. She is blessed to come from a large Southern family, and her fondest memories include listening to stories recounted around the dinner table. She was a lover of books from a young age, devouring tales of romance, danger and love. She soon started writing them herself. You can connect with Virginia through her website, virginiavaughanonline.com, or through the publisher.

Books by Virginia Vaughan

Love Inspired Suspense

Rangers Under Fire

Yuletide Abduction
Reunion Mission
Ranch Refuge
Mistletoe Reunion Threat
Mission Undercover
Mission: Memory Recall

No Safe Haven

MISSION: MEMORY RECALL

VIRGINIA VAUGHAN

⧫ HARLEQUIN® LOVE INSPIRED® SUSPENSE

Recycling programs for this product may not exist in your area.

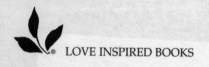

LOVE INSPIRED BOOKS

ISBN-13: 978-1-335-49014-8

Mission: Memory Recall

Copyright © 2018 by Virginia Vaughan

www.Harlequin.com

Printed in U.S.A.

Let us hold fast the profession of our faith without wavering; (for he is faithful that promised;)
—*Hebrews* 10:23

To Beverly, who left this world
before finding out how the story ended.

ONE

CIA Analyst Bethany Bryant's heart raced as she parked her rented SUV in a parking space in front of Milo's Diner in Little Falls, Texas. Taking out her gun, she checked it then slid it back into the holster beneath her jacket. She hoped she wouldn't have to use it, but she was ready in case she did. Her pulse was pounding with both excitement and angst.

She stared through the front windows of the diner and braced herself. For two years she'd been stalking a shadow across several countries and most recently to this sleepy little town. Social Security files showed employment activity at this diner on a false identity she'd been tracking as recently as two months ago. Now she was here and this place might finally hold the answers she'd been seeking for so long.

Bethany closed her eyes. She couldn't handle any more disappointments, any more false hopes. Taking a deep breath, she stared ahead and couldn't help wondering if her friend Dillon was right. He would tell her to face the facts—Marcus Allen was dead and she was chasing a figment of her imagination.

But it *could* be him.

Her heart kicked up a notch. She was also anxious about what would happen once she stepped inside the diner. How would she handle it if it was really him? She hoped she could keep her calm and professionalism, but a part of her was afraid she might cry like a little girl if she saw the face of the man who had haunted her dreams for so long. Drawing another deep, bracing breath, she got out of the vehicle, smoothed her long, dark ponytailed hair and her clothes then headed inside. She paused at the door and squared her shoulders before stepping through.

Milo's was an old-fashioned diner with stools at the counter and booths lining the walls. There was even an opening where one could see into the kitchen. The aroma of bacon and breakfast goods greeted her along with the familiar clanking of dishes and the chatter of conversation by the customers of the nearly full eatery. Bethany found an empty booth with a clear view of the kitchen and strained her head to try to see inside. She saw people, bodies, but no faces.

A pretty middle-aged woman with an apron and notebook approached her table and wiped it down. "Welcome to Milo's, hon. What can I getcha?"

"Just coffee, please," she stated, scanning the area behind the counter for a familiar face.

"We have a great breakfast special. Steak and eggs for only $5.99. Sure you're not hungry?"

"No, thank you. Just the coffee."

Laughter caught her attention and she gazed past the waitress and through the window into the kitchen. She knew that deep baritone voice. She'd heard it before, reveled in it. Her breath caught and a moment later her world shattered when she spotted the familiar strong jaw, green eyes and wide, bright smile through the opening.

Tears threatened her. He was alive. It was true. It was really true. Marcus Allen was alive. Then, as suddenly as that emotion had hit her, it morphed into anger. Marcus Allen was alive and working as a fry cook in a diner in Texas.

"Are you okay, honey?" the waitress asked. "You look kinda pale. Can I get you some water?"

"No, I'm fine. I was just caught off guard by the laughter. It sounded like someone I used to know."

The waitress turned and glanced into the kitchen. "You know Marcus?"

Ah, that was the real question, wasn't it? "I used to know him a long time ago."

The woman whose name badge read Marie turned and hollered toward the kitchen. "Marcus! This girl claims she knows you. Get out here and say hello."

Bethany's heart jerked as the man peered through the open window then waved. She pressed her arm against the gun under the jacket as she debated her own reaction. Her first instinct was to run to him, pull him into her arms and praise God for his safe return. She checked that. After all, she hardly recognized the man approaching her table.

Dressed in jeans, a T-shirt and cowboy boots, he

wore a long apron over his clothes and tossed a dish towel over his shoulder as he approached her. His eyes narrowed as he neared and he cocked his head as if trying to place her. Bethany felt herself go on alert. It *was* him! It was Marcus Allen walking and talking and cooking fried food.

She sucked in a breath and tried to get hold of her tangled emotions. If Marcus was alive, that meant… that meant he'd lied to the entire world. And now he was walking toward her as if nothing was out of the ordinary. He acted as if he didn't even know her and that made her mad all over again. She gritted her teeth, fury rushing through her. How could he not remember her? And if she shot him, could she really be charged with a crime?

After all, to the rest of the world, Marcus Allen had died two years ago in Afghanistan.

Excitement burst through Marcus as he approached the table where his boss and Milo's co-owner, Marie, stood with a pretty brunette. His adrenaline had started pumping the moment she'd called out to say someone knew him. He'd hoped to recognize the woman, but he didn't. Nothing registered.

He pushed back the disappointment. It didn't mean anything. He didn't even know himself these days, much less the beautiful woman with the long, dark hair and riveting blue eyes. He only knew his name was Marcus because the Afghani villagers who rescued him had called him that. He didn't even know for certain it was his name, but this woman knew. This woman knew *him*.

He sucked in a breath. Her gaze was hard as he approached, but he didn't stop. If she really knew who he was and this wasn't just a case of mistaken identity, then she had answers...answers he'd spent the past two years seeking.

The lovely stranger didn't flinch as he slid across from her in the booth and removed the wet towel from his shoulder. He eyed her, bracing himself for the unescapable moment when she would declare, "Sorry, I thought you were someone else."

"Hi," he said, his voice shaky with excitement. "Marie said you recognized me? I'm sorry, I don't recall your name."

Her eyes blazed at his words and he could see it made her mad that he didn't remember. What were the chances that he finally had contact with someone who could give him answers and she turned out to be an angry ex-girlfriend? Was he that kind of guy? The love-'em-and-leave-'em type? He. Just. Didn't. Know.

"Bethany," she stated through clenched teeth.

"I'm sorry I can't place you, Bethany. Something happened to me and I've been having a difficult time remembering things. Can I ask how you know me?"

She leaned forward and stared into his eyes, her gaze probing. He let her and didn't look away. It had to be weird having someone you knew not recognize you.

"Really, Marcus? You're really going to pretend to have amnesia?"

"I'm not pretending. Why would I make up something like that?"

"Because you're in a heap of trouble, that's why." She pulled out her wallet and opened it, revealing a federal identification badge.

"What does the CIA want with me?" he asked, feeling sweat break out on his forehead. This was what he'd been most afraid of, that if and when he finally discovered the truth about himself, he wouldn't like it very much. The villagers who'd cared for his wounds in Afghanistan had told him the CIA was hunting him. Her presence cemented that fear.

Just then his ears grabbed onto a familiar sound. He recognized the high-pitched whistling immediately and reacted. "Get down!" he hollered as something exploded through the window above their heads and the air filled with glass and a rush of stifling heat. Marcus hit the floor as bullets whizzed past him and slammed into the metal doors that led into the kitchen. Someone screamed and the panic-stricken patrons started running for the door. Marcus glanced at Bethany. She was crouched beside the table, her gun drawn and ready to return fire.

"Get down! Stay away from the windows!" Bethany screamed at the crowd as the bullets continued flying. She appeared ready to fight back, but it seemed awfully convenient that on the day she'd found him, someone was firing into the crowded diner.

The front doors were shoved open and several people spilled out onto the sidewalk. The shooter didn't target them as they fled, but who was to say he wouldn't start?

Marcus thought the guy's intent was probably to create pandemonium and, if it was, he'd been successful.

Moving to the metal doors already riddled with bullet holes, Marcus motioned for the rest of the crowd to rush toward the back. He noticed fear on their faces, yet he remained oddly calm under fire. How had he known that that sound had meant a bullet was headed their way? And why did this all seem second nature to him?

"Stay low and you'll be safe," he assured everyone as they began to filter back. Marcus spotted Milo huddled under the counter with Marie. He nodded at them. "Get those people into the freezer." The large walk-in was solidly built and would withstand the gunfire. He glanced back at the holes in the door and knew instinctively that this wasn't a random shooting. He was the target.

Milo kept a rifle under the counter in case of trouble. Marcus tore off his apron, crawled across the floor and reached to the back, his hand grabbing metal. He checked the weapon, glad to see it was loaded. *Thank you, Milo.*

He looked at Bethany. She wasn't backing down, either. In fact, she was crouched on a leather booth seat, gun by her hand and using a mirrored compact to try to get a better look at the shooter.

Marcus joined her at the booth. "See anything?"

"Only one shooter. Looks like he's perched on the top of the bank building across the street."

"That's a perfect vantage point for a sniper. He fired a lot of shots but didn't hit anyone in the crowd. He must have been trying to create panic. Any chance he's one of yours?"

"You mean CIA? No. No one from the Agency knew I was coming. I've been tracking you off the books." She pulled out her phone and dialed 9-1-1. "Someone is shooting into Milo's Diner on Main Street. We need police and ambulance response pronto."

He jumped up, pushed the shotgun through the window and fired. Bethany fired, too, and the sniper stopped shooting for only a moment before Marcus spotted the red laser that indicated the assailant had turned on his targeting gear. It swept the area, trying to find its mark as Marcus and Bethany crept out of its range.

"We're not going to stop him from here," he stated. This all felt so natural and, once again, that struck him as odd. He'd done this sort of thing before. He was certain of it. He grimaced. If this sniper hadn't showed up, he would already have the answers he needed from the pretty brunette. He clutched his gun. She *knew* him. She knew *him*. The idea both baffled and amazed him.

"We've got to go out there and stop him. We can go out the back then circle around the hardware store and climb up the back of the building."

She nodded, agreeing, and he was glad because he was going to make sure they didn't get separated. This Fed had the answers to the questions he'd been seeking. He wasn't letting her out of his sight.

Bethany followed him into the kitchen. The freezer door opened and Milo peeked out.

"Is it safe?" he asked. "It's cold in here."

Marcus waved him away. "Get back inside. Better to be cold than dead. The police are on the way."

"And what are you two doing?"

"We're going after the sniper. Keep everyone inside until they arrive."

While some people had gotten away and he'd noticed the shooter hadn't targeted them, it was too dangerous to allow anyone else out. They were better off staying in the freezer for now until the police arrived.

Marcus went out the back door and, crouching against the wall, followed the building to the front. He was hyperaware that Bethany was right behind him.

He cautiously glanced out and the sniper fired. He jumped back. "He's got us pinned down. How many bullets do you have left in that gun?"

She pulled it to her in a protective manner. "Enough. Why?"

"You draw his fire. I'll circle around the back of the hardware store and confront him."

She frowned and he could see she didn't like the thought of letting him out of her sight, but what choice did she really have?

Finally, after several long moments, she reluctantly nodded, but then obviously felt the need to clarify something. "You'd better not disappear again, Marcus. I found you once. I'll find you again."

He was certain she could but her worry was in vain. "I'm not going anywhere." He'd come here to find answers and she was the first clue to his identity. He wasn't going to run from her now.

She braced herself then started firing at the building. Marcus took off running, crossing the street then ducking into the hardware store. Mr. Bennett, the store's owner, was hunkered down behind the counter.

Shouldering his rifle, Marcus told him to stay low as he hurried to the back, swooping up a rope from a shelf before exiting through the door. He quickly knotted the rope and then tossed it up the side of the building until it caught. He scaled the side of the building, all the while conscious of Bethany's firing to keep the sniper engaged.

Good girl. Keep him occupied.

The rope burned into his hands but he didn't stop. Hefting himself over the top of the roof, once again he was acutely aware of the fact that he'd done this before.

The scream of sirens wailed in the distance and Marcus knew the police would arrive soon enough, more likely new targets of the sniper's aim. He needed to get over there and find out just who was shooting at them before further chaos erupted.

But he also needed to get back to the woman who held the answers to all his questions. *You've brought me this far, Lord. You sent this Federal Agent with knowledge of my past to find me. Please don't let anything happen before I can hear what she has to say.*

He drew his gun and moved across the rooftop, every muscle on alert as he ran to the edge.

He scanned the rooftop quickly, spotting a rifle leaning against the wall, but the shooter was gone.

Suddenly someone grabbed him from behind, pulling something hard and tight against him. Marcus caught it with his hand, knowing that if the attacker managed to get this around his neck, he was done for.

And everyone else down there would have to deal with this guy alone. He couldn't allow that.

Marcus summoned more strength than he knew he had, reached back to grab the guy and then slung him across his shoulder. He hit the ground with a thud and a groan while Marcus scrambled to stay on his feet at the near loss of air supply.

Air Supply. He loved the band Air Supply.

He shook his head. *Stop it and focus. Fight now. Answers later.*

His attacker was dressed all in black, his face hidden by goggles and a sand scarf. It was a look familiar to Marcus; the guy resembled a bandit from the Old West. Marcus himself had dressed like that before for undercover work.

Unfortunately, his attacker didn't stay down. He leaped to his feet, ready to attack again.

Marcus faced him, unable to shake the familiar look of him. He couldn't see his face because of the sand scarf and goggles, but he knew the look, the stance, even the weapon of choice—a .300 Win Mag sniper rifle. Powerful and precise enough to shoot across a long distance. In other words, the perfect sniper's rifle.

The masked figure lunged and Marcus engaged him, surprised to find he matched him move for move. He acted on instinct, the efforts coming naturally to him. He didn't even have to think which move to make because his muscles seemed to know before his mind did. Finally, the assailant drop-kicked him and Marcus hit the ground and rolled. When he turned over to get to his feet, his attacker lowered his gun and held it to his head.

"You should have stayed dead, Marcus," the clad figure stated.

But before he could shoot, another gun fired, this time from behind him. The bullet didn't hit him but he jerked and spun around to face the new shooter from his spot on the ground.

Marcus spotted striking blue eyes belonging to none other than Bethany, the CIA agent, her weapon raised and firing. Man, she was gorgeous. The attacker hopped over the side of the building and vanished. She raced to the edge and looked over as Marcus crawled to his feet.

She turned back to him, irritation glowering on her face. "He's gone."

"Apparently so." Marcus walked to the perch where the sniper had left his weapon and gear. He glanced through the scope. The diner had indeed been the target. But why and who had targeted them?

He heard the click of a gun safety releasing behind him. "Get away from that."

He glanced back and saw Bethany with her gun now aimed at him.

"I'm just checking it out."

"I said move away from it," she insisted, so he did. If she wanted to play things her way then he would let her for now.

Lowering her weapon, she picked up the sniper rifle and glanced through the scope.

"The diner was the target. Or rather, someone inside the diner." She picked up the gear bag and dug through it. "There's no identification."

"He wouldn't have any," Marcus offered and she

glanced up at him with those probing eyes. "Despite what people commonly believe, snipers don't work alone. They need someone to watch the wind and environment as well as, in this case, people coming to intercept them. In this case, if he hadn't been working alone, he never would have left his stuff behind. We're looking for a single sniper."

"I'm familiar with sniper protocols," she snapped, a comment that made him wonder why he was familiar with them. Had he been a sniper?

The person to ask was standing in front of him and there was no time like the present. After all, he'd made this journey to find answers.

"Back at the diner, you told Marie you knew me. Was that true? Do you know who I am?"

She looked up at him, surprise shining in her eyes. He held his breath. This was the moment he'd waited for, prayed for, even trekked across the Middle East for.

She straightened and raised her gun at him again, this time startling him enough to cause him to take several steps back.

"I do know you. You're Marcus Allen. And you're under arrest for treason and desertion."

Bethany saw surprise color his face and felt more vindicated than she had since she'd first realized he hadn't died that night in Afghanistan.

"I think you're making a mistake," he stated. "You're seriously arresting me?"

Technically, she didn't have the authority to arrest him, but she could and would detain him until he could be placed in custody. And, officially, she knew there were no active arrest warrants for Marcus Allen because as far as the US government was concerned, he'd died in Afghanistan two years ago.

"I know exactly who you are. I've been tracking you for the past two years." She took out her CIA credentials and flashed them once again. "You're on the government's radar." Maybe she was overstepping her bounds here. Technically, he was only on her radar, but he didn't need to know that.

He looked downtrodden. "I'm a criminal? I thought when you told Marie you knew me, that you actually *knew* me." He glanced at her derisively. "You're nothing but an agent looking for her next prey."

She sighed and lowered the gun. "You're being a little melodramatic, aren't you, Marcus? Of course I know you." He'd made certain he'd be remembered when he'd made her fall in love with him then run out on her and everyone else.

The bitterness of realizing she'd been duped still stung Bethany because she had fallen for Marcus. She'd fallen hard for the handsome soldier with the broad smile and easygoing manner. The few weeks they'd spent together before the ambush had been the best of her life and she'd been just as devastated when she'd thought he'd died only to discover she'd been used as a means to an end.

Her face radiated heat at the reminder of the fool she'd been for him. She'd cried for this man when she'd thought he died! Then to discover he'd not only survived but had had a hand in the ambush had nearly done her in. Only her anger and quest for revenge had kept her going. Now he was standing in front of her and, more than wanting to know why he'd betrayed his country, she wanted to demand to know why he'd betrayed *her*. But she couldn't focus on that now. That wasn't the important part of why she'd tracked him down. Betraying his country was by far the more critical issue.

"What have I done that the CIA is hunting me?"

"You're a US soldier who went missing and was presumed killed in action. I have a duty to bring you in through the proper channels. Everyone is going to want to talk to you, to hear your story."

"But I don't know my story." He grunted and spun away from her, his shoulders tense. "How can I tell anyone what happened when I don't know myself what went down?" He turned back, looked at her and shook his head. "But you don't believe me, do you?"

"That you have amnesia?" she scoffed. "Come on, Marcus, drop the act. We both know you've been in hiding for nearly two years."

"I wasn't hiding."

"Whatever it was, I'm taking you in. The only question is how we're going to do this."

He saw her clutch the gun then hung his head and sighed. "You won't need that." He held out the rifle in his hand to her, butt first. "I'm not a fugitive and I'm certainly not dangerous."

"But you *are* under arrest. Let's go. You'll pay for the crimes you've committed against your country."

"I have no idea what you're talking about. I—I don't even know—"

His lack of recognition hurt more than she cared to admit, but she didn't let it show. "What? You don't recognize me? That's fine, Marcus, but I certainly remember you."

"All I know is I woke up injured, with no memory of how it happened or who I was. The only reason I know my name is because the people who cared for me told me they overheard others calling me Marcus." Exhaling roughly, he rubbed a hand across his face. "They told me the CIA was after me, so I went into hiding, but I couldn't stand the hiding anymore. I came here trying to find answers to who I am and what happened to me. Then you showed up and the shooting started."

Bethany was about to call him out on his fanciful tale, but the sincerity in his face stopped her again. Before she had a moment to steel herself from his eyes, the rooftop door burst open and six men dressed in local police attire, with weapons raised, stormed onto the roof.

"Stop right there," one of them called. "Drop your weapon and step away from it."

She did as the officer commanded and sank to the ground, carefully placing her gun on the rooftop. It was better to cooperate with the authorities because she knew they would eventually get everything sorted out. Marcus, too, raised his hands over his head and followed the officer's instructions.

"My name is Bethany Bryant," she called out. "I'm an agent with the CIA. If you'll look in my jacket pocket, you'll find my credentials and identification." She'd given up field work for a desk job after the ambush in which she'd thought Marcus had died, but still maintained her field agent status.

The officer who searched her glanced at her CIA credentials then passed them along to his boss, who nodded and ordered her released. "We were responding to shots fired into the diner. Can you tell us what happened here?"

"I've been tracking this man on charges of treason and terrorist activities. I'd just made contact when the shooting started. It looks like someone was trying to take him out before he could talk to me. I'd like to have him placed in a jail cell and under close guard to await the arrival of Federal Marshals to transport him to Langley to stand trial. And, be careful, he's highly trained and skilled in matters of combat."

Bethany watched his face as the officers led him away. He looked resigned to being arrested. He didn't struggle when they cuffed him or moved him along.

She was right beside him when the local police walked him through town and the man and woman from the diner approached, expressions of worry lining their faces. "Marcus? What's going on? What's happening? Why are they arresting you?"

"It's okay, Milo. It's all a big mistake."

Marie approached Bethany and grabbed her arm. "Why are you arresting Marcus? You saw, he was the one who was helping get people to safety when the shots started. He's a good guy."

Bethany pulled her arm away. "I'm sorry, but you have no idea what kind of man Marcus Allen really is."

She saw the looks of doubt on their faces. They didn't

believe her, but she didn't hold it against them. She knew personally how easy it was to be fooled into thinking Marcus Allen was one of the good guys.

TWO

Sheriff Ken Mills was a burly man who epitomized the stereotypical small-town Texas sheriff. But he sat and listened—staring at Bethany's credentials instead of looking directly at her—while she explained the situation and asked for his help. Technically, he didn't have to offer any assistance to her since the CIA wasn't supposed to be operating on US soil, but most law-enforcement agencies shared so many common experiences that camaraderie was generally expected and usually given.

When she was finished, Mills leaned back in his chair and surveyed her. "I'll agree to this on several conditions, Agent Bryant. One, you don't interfere with our investigation into the shooting and, two, you offer up any and all information you know about it."

She nodded. "Of course. I will." That was a given.

"How long do you think you'll need to house this prisoner of yours in our facility?"

"Not long at all. One night. Maybe two at the most."

"Fine. My last condition is that my detectives want to question him about what he knows about the shooting without interference from you or the Agency. I don't want to hear that we can't solve a shooting in our own community because the CIA deems it sensitive information."

"I don't think that's going to be a problem, Sheriff. In fact, I would love to be kept informed about any information your detectives garner from Marcus."

"I'll let them know." He stood and shook her hand. "It's hard to believe that we had a fugitive from the CIA living right here in our community and no one knew it. Keep us updated and we'll do the same."

She left his office and was met by Detective Mercer, who told her they were still going through evidence and wouldn't be talking with Marcus for several more hours.

Bethany took the opportunity to dial the number for Rick Eaves, her CIA department supervisor, to update him. When he answered, she spilled the news about finding Marcus.

She heard his sharp intake of breath. "Marcus Allen? You really found him?"

"I did. He's alive. He was working as a fry cook in a town called Little Falls, Texas."

"I'm in shock, Bethany. I confess I thought you were just chasing shadows. Are you certain it's him? Maybe it's just someone who looks like him."

She remembered staring up into Marcus's achingly familiar green eyes and mentally shook her head. She would never forget his face. "It's him. I'm certain of it."

"Okay, then we need to plan our next move. Do you want me to call in a team to bring him in?"

She'd gone against Agency protocols by not calling in a fugitive recovery team. But then, she hadn't been acting in an official capacity, either. "That's not necessary."

"This is a dangerous man, Bethany. He's been on the run for years. There's no telling what he might do if you confront him."

She grimaced, bracing for his reaction. "I already have."

"You did *what*? Are you insane? You know our standard operating procedures for capturing fugitives."

She couldn't help the indignation that arose inside her. No one had believed her and now she was catching flack for being right. "I wasn't operating under an official capacity, remember? I didn't think I had the resources of the Agency to help with this."

Rick took a deep breath as if realizing she was right and then continued in a calmer tone. "What happened?"

"Nothing. He claims to have amnesia. He says he doesn't even know me."

"Amnesia? Are you seriously buying that?"

She wanted to assure her supervisor she didn't, but the image of Marcus's green eyes looking at her so earnestly for answers as he'd sat across from her flashed through her mind and she couldn't form the words. So instead of responding to his question, she moved on to the next issue. "We have another pressing problem. A sniper fired into the diner just after I approached him."

"They're trying to kill him before he can talk to us."

Her mind spun at that notion. "Who is trying to kill him?"

"Bethany, you don't think he's been on his own all

this time, do you? He must have been working with someone to stay under the radar."

She didn't bother reminding him that Marcus hadn't managed to stay under her radar. "I haven't gotten to officially interrogate him yet, but I will soon."

"You do that. I'm going to start making preparations to get you both back here as soon as possible. I'll call the Marshals' office. I assume the locals will hold him until they arrive?"

"Yes, I've already spoken to the sheriff. He wants answers about this shooting just as much as we do."

"Don't let them take over. He's our prisoner, not theirs. Make sure they know that. Do you want me to call the sheriff?"

"That's not necessary. I can handle it."

"Okay. I'll be in touch once the arrangements for the Marshals are under way."

She hung up but instead of feeling proud of herself for finally capturing Marcus after all these years, she felt as if she'd just been scolded by her supervisor. And it rankled because she'd accomplished something no one else at the Agency had been able to do.

Rick Eaves and the rest of the CIA had underestimated her and now she'd proved them all wrong.

She should have felt vindicated. So why then did it feel like her heart was breaking?

The local cops paraded him inside like a common criminal. He didn't like it, but he allowed it because Bethany was right about people wanting to question him. And maybe they could help him recover some of his memories.

Their sheriff offered his help and had a deputy escort Marcus to a jail cell. He sat on the cold, hard seat and waited. None of this had gone as he'd anticipated. He'd certainly not expected to be sitting in a county jail awaiting transport to CIA headquarters.

He closed his eyes and lifted a prayer to God. Surely, He hadn't brought him all this way to make him a prisoner. Bethany had called him a traitor to his country. He didn't feel like one, but how could he really know for sure?

Flashes of the past hit him. Gunfire and running. Pain bursting through him. A woman staring up at him, awaiting a kiss— He jolted awake at that last image, realizing he'd dozed off. The woman reminded him of Bethany, like it could have been her sister, but her eyes had been different, a deep brown color instead of the vivid blue, and her face and hair had been hidden under a tunic. But the resemblance was uncanny. He wiped his face, trying to rub away some of the fogginess that clouded his memories.

"What are you thinking about so intently, Marcus?" Her voice came this time not from his memory but from behind the wall of bars separating them. Her eyes were once again their bright glory blue.

"You, actually." He stood and approached her. She held the answers to all his questions. "How do we know each other? I mean, I know you're a CIA agent hunting me, but are we more than that?"

She chewed on her bottom lip in a telling fashion. "Why would you ask me that question?"

"I keep seeing this woman flashing before my eyes."

"So you admit you remember me?"

"I guess I do. It's just a glimmer, but I remember seeing you." *And kissing you.* What was that about? "But the woman looked different…the eyes?"

Bethany gave a weary sigh. "They're called contact lenses, Marcus. You know very well that I wear them when I'm on assignment."

Her words flowed back to him, words she'd spoken years and several thousand miles ago. "Because who would believe an Afghani woman with blue eyes?"

She stared up at him, those same eyes flashing with anger. "So you *do* remember?"

He rubbed his eyes, pain shooting through his head as he tried to concentrate. "I don't know. Maybe." He saw the doubt on her face. "I'm not lying to you, Bethany. My past is a blank slate. You have no idea how frustrating that is. I remember how to walk, talk, drive a car, shoot a gun, but when I try to recall who I am or where I come from or what I've done, there's nothing."

"We'll see. The CIA has methods to obtain information."

"I'm sure they do."

She waved her hand at the camera and the electronic lock released. "I have a few of my own methods right now. Will you follow me to the interview room?"

He allowed her to cuff him and lead him down the long hallway then turn right into an interrogation room.

When they entered, Marcus saw what looked to be the content from the shooter's nest.

"What's all this?" he asked.

She motioned toward the weapon. "You tell me. Everything has been unloaded, of course."

"Of course." He picked up the rifle and checked the mag. "This is a .300 Win Mag sniper rifle with long-range scope. The most accurate sniper's rifle on the market." He glanced at the other equipment on the table. It was all top-quality gear. "Aside from the working on his own part, I'd say our sniper is a professional assassin."

She nodded. "I agree. And you let him get away. Who's after you, Marcus?"

He sighed, already weary of her not believing him, and sank into a chair. "Why do you think he was after me? You were in that diner, too, as were a handful of patrons. Any one of them could have been the target."

"That's highly unlikely. You're a fugitive on the run. I feel certain you were the mark. Besides, he didn't target anyone else as they were fleeing the building, only you."

"Well, I haven't been targeted until today. Believe me, nothing like this has happened to me before you arrived in town. I was hoping you could provide me answers, but it seems you provided a lot more than that."

Anger flashed on her face. "Are you implying that I led someone to you who wanted you dead?"

She stood and walked to him, opening a folder. "Are you aware that all but six of your army ranger team died in an ambush in Afghanistan two years ago? All including you…or so everyone believed." She leaned over him, speaking directly into his ear. "You had us all fooled, Marcus. They all thought you'd died that night on that mountain. These men were your teammates, your friends."

He glanced at the file. "I didn't lie to anyone," he insisted.

"Then tell me what happened over there."

He dug through his memory, but only flashes came. Firefights. Cries of pain. And the soft skin of lips caressing his. She was all jumbled up in there, but even those fragments didn't provide the answers he needed. "I—I don't know. All I know is I was injured. The first thing I remember clearly was waking up in a hut. The villagers took care of me and treated my wounds. They sheltered me. But they kept saying I was in danger, that someone was hunting me, that someone in the CIA was after me."

"Why weren't they afraid of you? The CIA was the good guy."

"They didn't think so. They seemed frightened, so I was frightened, as well. I figured they were the ones who knew the good guys from the bad guys."

"Why didn't you report to a US military base? You would have been safe there."

"I had no idea who I was. For all I knew, I was on the run from the US government. I thought I would be arrested, or worse, killed."

She gave him a disgusted look and shook her head. "You have a US army ranger's tattoo on your left shoulder. No one could mistake that. You had a duty to return to the base when you were able and let someone know you were alive."

He pulled up his sleeve and showed her his shoulder. There was no army ranger tattoo, but the scarred flesh suggested that something had once been there. He'd never thought about it being a tattoo of any kind. Had just chalked the scarred flesh up to his injuries. Had someone burned off his tattoo to keep him safe? "I depended on those people to keep me alive. I did as I was told. Besides, they were right. The CIA was after me."

She stood and gathered the items, placing them back into an evidence container. "Tomorrow, the US Marshals will arrive to transport you back to CIA headquarters, where you'll be fully briefed about what happened the night of the ambush. There will be a lot of questions about how you survived and why you haven't come forward. I suggest you come up with a better story than this amnesia one."

"I can't tell you anything that isn't the truth, Beth."

She stopped, turned and glared at him. "You don't get to call me that."

Her words held a bite that chilled him. He'd hurt her. Badly. In his heart, he knew it hadn't been on purpose, but how could he prove it? How could he exonerate himself from a jail cell?

"I'm sorry." He spoke softly. "I don't mean to cause you more pain. I don't know how to prove to you that I'm not lying, but I promise you I'm not."

She folded her arms and gave him a stern look. "You may have made a fool of me, but don't worry, Marcus, you never hurt me."

She opened the door and called to a guard who grabbed him by the arm. He couldn't miss the pain simmering behind her eyes as he was led out of the room and back to lockup.

She was in her hotel room when her phone rang and she looked at the screen. It was Dillon Montgomery, her former partner in the CIA. They'd worked many operations together, including the one they'd been on when the ambush occurred. Dillon was one of the few agents in her division who hadn't forgotten about her when she'd accepted a desk job and he was the only one who still called her regularly and tried to encourage her back to field work.

She noticed she'd had several missed calls from him. She pressed the on button. "Dillon, hi."

"Where are you? I've been phoning you all day. I was starting to get worried."

These days, it was nothing for her to wake up to a text or email from Dillon that he was going on assignment. He could be called to a mission at a moment's notice and be gone for days or weeks. Bethany knew the routine well—she used to live it. But since she'd stopped doing field work, her job kept her closer to home, so her disappearing without a word was considered unusual by Dillon.

"I'm in Texas," she told him. "I decided to take a few days off."

The hesitation before he responded meant he knew why. Her obsession with finding Marcus was a constant source of tension between the two of them. Dillon had been the only one in the department to encourage her to follow her gut when it came to her investigation into Marcus. Everyone else had considered her obsession with finding him nothing more than a hopeless pursuit. But even Dillon's encouragement had waned recently.

"When are you going to give this up, Bethany?"

"I'm not giving up, Dillon. In fact, I found who I came looking for."

"What do you mean you found him?" His voice perked up. "Are you serious? Marcus Allen? You found him? Are you sure?"

"I am. It's definitely him."

He gave a low whistle. "Unbelievable. You always believed it, Bethany, even when the rest of us tried to dissuade you. Impressive. I'm so proud of you."

"Thank you, Dillon. I still can't believe I found him after all this time."

"A soldier presumed killed in action discovered alive? I, for one, can't wait to hear his story."

"Well, there won't be much of a story. He has amnesia."

Dillon snickered. "Amnesia? *Really?*"

"That's what he's claiming. Right after I confronted him, someone started shooting at us. He insists he has no idea why someone would try to kill him and no knowledge of who the sniper is."

"Of course he would say that," Dillon stated. "He's wanted by more than the CIA."

She frowned. Rick had alluded to something like that, too. "What do you mean?"

He laughed. "Come on, Bethany. What do you think

he's been doing all this time? He must have been work-ing for someone. Probably weapons traders, if I had my guess. If he's back in the States and someone is trying to kill him, he probably betrayed them, too."

"But why did they wait until I arrived to take those shots?" she asked. "Were they following me? Did I lead the shooter to him?"

Dillon gave a disgruntled sigh. "I doubt anyone in the CIA was following you around on the off chance you found a presumed-dead army ranger."

When he said it, it sounded so implausible that she blushed even thinking it.

"And who else would know about your investigation? I don't mean to put you down, Bethany, because you did it, you found Marcus Allen. But your investigation into this matter has been like a wild-goose chase. No one in the Agency or any other government agency gave your conclusions any merit. Certainly there was no one here waiting around to see if you found him."

He was only stating what she already knew to be true. It was silly to even think differently. Marcus was a target and had been for a while. He'd probably gone into hiding to begin with because someone was after him and thus had been dodging bullets for years. That certainly made more sense than that she'd led some-one to him. She grimaced to think she'd let him plant doubt in her mind.

"Of course. You're right."

"Tell me where you are," Dillon said. "I'll hop a flight and be there in a few hours to help you bring him in."

"That's not necessary. I've already made arrangements. He's being held in the local jail and Rick has ar-
ranged for the US Marshals to escort us back to Langley
tomorrow morning."

"Are you sure? I don't mind making the trip."

"No, it's fine. I'll see you when I return."

"Okay…have a safe trip," he said. "I'll see you when
you get back. We'll celebrate this victory. Steaks on the
grill at my place. Sound good?"

"That sounds nice."

"Seriously, Bethany. Good job."

She felt her face redden. She and Dillon had become
very close over the past year. He'd indicated he wanted
more than to be just friends but she'd put him off several times. She just didn't believe she was ready for that
even though deep down she knew he was a great guy.

He was handsome and charming and one of the more
successful agents in the terrorism division. They were
well matched and she knew the job often caused trouble in marriages, but marrying a fellow agent meant
being with someone who understood the job. And he
was the one who continually encouraged Bethany to
return to the field.

She hung up with Dillon, still pondering the state of
their relationship. She'd spent months putting him off
because of her obsession with finding Marcus. Now
that's she'd done it, was it time to give Dillon the attention he deserved?

She sighed.

The truth was that she'd never felt the spark with Dillon that she'd felt with Marcus. She knew it was silly to feel this way. Dillon was perfect for her.

She reddened again, remembering that what she'd felt for Marcus had been fabricated. It hadn't been real, only a con she'd fallen for.

That was enough. It was time to stop focusing on Marcus. She took some satisfaction in knowing she'd been right…that she'd been vindicated. Now her life of living in limbo was over. Though, what did that mean exactly? She'd spent so much time and energy hunting for Marcus that it had consumed her life for the past two years. It would take a while to adjust to her new normal.

Blowing out a breath, she grabbed her keys and headed out to her SUV. She wasn't going to sleep tonight because she was too keyed up. She might as well go over the evidence obtained from the rooftop. Because if someone else was after Marcus, as she suspected, they would have a fight on their hands to keep him out of harm's way.

When Bethany parked her SUV in the parking lot of the police station and got out, she was immediately approached by Marie and Milo.

"Why did you have Marcus arrested?" Marie demanded. "He wasn't the one shooting. He was helping people get to safety."

Bethany could see their deep concern for their employee. He'd obviously made an impression on them, but then, he was good at getting people to trust him then running out on them. She decided they needed to know who it was they were putting such faith in.

"I'm sorry to be the one to tell you this, but he's not the man you think he is."

"He told us all about his past…or rather that he didn't know his past."

Bethany narrowed her eyes at them. "He told you he didn't know who he was yet you hired him, anyway?"

Milo nodded. "He needed help. That was obvious. We met him when he first arrived in town. He attended a service at our church. He seemed lost and alone, but a decent fellow. At first we gave him small jobs around the diner but he kept going above and beyond what was asked of him. We soon realized he was a decent, hard worker, and wanted to know more about him, so we had him over to supper." He took a breath. "That's when he told us about the amnesia and how he was looking for answers about his life. We encouraged him to stay here in town and let us help him."

"And you truly believe he can't remember his past?"

"Sure. Why would he lie about something like that?"

"When you said you knew him, I was thrilled," Marie stated. "I couldn't wait to tell him. Now I'm regretting that a little bit. I had no idea you would arrest him."

"You said yourself you had no idea who he was or what he'd done. You can't be too shocked to discover he was on the run."

"No, ma'am. No idea," Milo reiterated. "That boy was trying to be found by someone. He contacted the news station in Dallas, hoping they could spread his story around but the producers wouldn't help him. Apparently, it didn't make good news. He also had the local

PD fingerprint him and run his prints, but they came back without a match."

Bethany wasn't surprised about the fingerprints. Military files weren't usually included in local print searches. Those were generally limited to the criminal databases. But she was shocked to hear Marcus had made attempts to try to be identified. What sort of game was he playing?

"So am I the first who's come looking for him? Have there been other instances like the one today?"

"Not a one. As far as we know, he'd never been to Little Falls before. He just ended up here. We never expected this. Marcus arrived in town seven months ago and nothing like this has happened. Are you sure the person who was doing the shooting was after him?"

"Who else would he be after?"

"Well, you're CIA, aren't you? Don't you people have enemies?"

Bethany wanted to quickly reassure Marie that this shooting had nothing to do with her, but she tamped down the thought before she voiced it and said instead, "We're investigating all possibilities." She hadn't done field work except for her time spent tracking Marcus since the night of the ambush. She'd immediately requested and been granted a desk analysis job. It wasn't unusual for agents to opt out of field work for a brief time, but her reprieve had turned into a permanent position a long time ago. No one except Dillon had brought up the idea of her going out into the field in over nine months' time. And the chances that someone was targeting her on the exact day she'd located Marcus seemed much too impossible to be true. Marcus had to have been the target of that sniper's bullet.

She turned her focus away from the incident and to the couple in front of her. They'd been around since this morning and it was now pushing 8:00 p.m. Had they been here all day waiting on news for someone they hardly knew? "What are you two still doing here?" she asked. "Visiting hours have been over for quite a while."

"We brought something for Marcus, only that Patrolman Dwight won't let us see him to give it to him."

"Well, he's not really allowed any outside belongings."

"But surely his Bible isn't included in that," Marie proclaimed. She reached into her bag and pulled out a large, well-worn, leather Bible. "I know for a fact he reads from it every night without fail. Maybe you could get it to him?"

The pleading in the woman's voice was something Bethany couldn't ignore. "I suppose I can."

"Thank you," she said as she handed it over.

Bethany watched the couple load into a pickup, wave and then drive away. She stared at the Bible in her hands. Was this really Marcus's Bible? When she'd known him, he hadn't been religious.

She flipped through the pages and noticed writings and markings with notes in the margins. Whoever this belonged to had used it, studied it. She shook her head. Another thing about this entire situation that didn't seem to make any sense. As she turned to go into the jail, a piece of paper slipped through the pages and landed on the ground. She knelt to pick it up. The paper, too, was well-worn, but it wasn't a page from the Bible. It was a napkin with a drawing of a woman's face…a woman with long hair and full lips, in head garb. She recognized it immediately.

The drawing was of her.

Anger burned through her. He claimed not to remember her and now she'd found something like this? But if his feelings for her hadn't been real, then why the ploy to pretend he cared about her?

The events of the day had left her confused and frustrated. Nothing about all this made sense and she was beginning to wish she'd never discovered Marcus was still alive.

Bethany walked inside, past the on-duty officer—the skinny guy named Dwight who wouldn't allow Marie inside with the Bible. He was the only one on duty and was engrossed in something on his computer.

"This place really shuts down at night, doesn't it?" she asked him.

He nodded her way. "We don't have much activity downtown at night. We usually only keep one or two officers in the precinct while the rest patrol."

She thought about what Marie and Milo told her about Marcus's attempts to discover his identity but hesitated asking Dwight about it. Finally she voiced the question. She did need to cover all her bases. "Officer Dwight, before I arrived in town today, did Marcus ask anyone around here to fingerprint him?"

"I heard he asked the sheriff about running his prints because he said he couldn't remember his name, but I don't think anything turned up."

"Do you know if they ran his prints through the military system?"

"I don't know. I wasn't on duty at the time."

She thanked Dwight then walked down to the jail area and pressed the automated button that opened the door. Marcus was the only prisoner. The hall was dark but she spotted a small light in the back cell so she knew Marcus was still up. When she approached the cell, she was shocked to see him on his knees, by his cot, head bowed and praying.

The image caught her off guard and she suddenly felt like an intruder. Through the bars, she placed the Bible on the shelf then turned and left, leaving him alone in the private moment.

A feeling of unease coursed through her. She should have been resting easily having proved once and for all that Marcus Allen was alive and that all the suspicions she'd had were true. But her mind was working overtime, trying to process everything, but the events of today were like pieces of different jigsaw puzzles. Was it possible Marcus was telling her the truth? That he'd suffered amnesia and had no idea what had happened to him the night of the ambush?

Bethany closed her eyes and sighed wearily. She'd thought when she'd found him, everything would finally make sense.

Now, nothing did.

She walked back into the bull pen and approached Dwight. "I'd like to go through the evidence gathered today on the rooftop." She'd watched Dwight bag and tag each item earlier and place it inside the locked evidence cabinet for safe keeping.

"It's kind of late, isn't it?"

"Not for me."

He shrugged, pushed to his feet and headed for the evidence locker, keys in hand.

Bethany followed behind him and watched as he pressed the key into the lock. It gave without turning and she immediately saw him tense.

"The lock is busted." He pulled open the cabinet door.

The shelves were empty.

The sniper's rifle and all the evidence of the rooftop shoot-out were gone.

THREE

The quiet of the jail cell was interrupted by the sound of footsteps. But it wasn't the sound of someone approaching that caught Marcus's attention. It was how quiet they were trying to be. All his senses went on alert and the hairs on his neck stood up.

He pushed off the cot where he'd been sleeping and walked to the door of the cell. He scanned the corridor for movement. The only light stemmed from the bulb filtering in through the door into the precinct. He could turn on his own light, but he sensed it would spook whoever was there...and he wanted to know who it was trying to sneak up on him.

He pushed back against the side of the cell, out of sight of the door. A shadow appeared, jutting a rifle barrel between the bars. Before he could fire, Marcus grabbed it and yanked, slamming the would-be shooter hard into the bars. To his credit, he didn't release the weapon but shoved back. The cell door swung open, jerking Marcus out of the cell. It was unlocked. The electronic locks would have to have been unlocked by someone in the bull pen, so either this attacker was working with someone or had planned ahead and unlocked them himself.

He grabbed Marcus around the neck and tightened his grip. Marcus gasped for air and felt his knees about to buckle in the strong hold. If he lost consciousness, he would be killed for sure. He gripped the man's arms then strained with every ounce of strength he had. His survival instincts kicking into high gear, he shoved backward, slamming his attacker hard against the wall. He heard him grunt, but his grip didn't loosen. At least, not the first time.

Marcus rammed him again and again until the gun slipped from the assailant's hand and hit the floor. Marcus pulled free and dove for the gun, but the guy reached it first and started firing blindly. Sparks of light flickered at each gunshot and the sound was deafening.

Without a weapon, Marcus had little chance of defending himself. He ran for the door at the end of the corridor and nearly fell back when it swung open and Bethany stood there with her gun raised. She saw Marcus, motioned for him to slide past her then started firing blindly into the hall.

Marcus ran through the door and hit the switch to turn on the overhead lights. They took several moments to come on and by the time they did, the corridor was empty.

He heard Bethany's heavy breathing as she took several steps forward. She knew, as he did, that the shooter hadn't gotten past them through the only door out of the place. He had to be hiding inside one of the cells.

Marcus motioned at the first cell and she nodded and moved toward it, but before she reached it, he spotted the jutting muzzle of a gun.

"Gun!" he yelled, grabbing Bethany and pulling her through the door just as the shooter began firing again. He leaped to his feet and pulled her up with him. "Run."

She nodded and took off running and he followed her through the empty police bull pen.

"My SUV is parked out front," she stated, never stopping.

He considered grabbing a weapon from the police stash but she shook her head. "Forget it, Marcus, they're gone. Everything is gone. Dwight went out to the car to secure a weapon and call for backup when I heard the shooting start."

He had only a half second to ponder her words before the door squeaked open and he heard footsteps again, this time heavy and quick.

"Our only choice is to get out of here." Gesturing for him to follow, Bethany burst through the outer doors and into the nearly empty parking lot. She ran to her SUV. He was right behind her, slipping inside moments before she started the engine and jammed it into gear then roared away.

He glanced back and saw the dark figure emerge from the station and raise his weapon to fire. But the shots never came. Instead the assailant lowered the gun, obviously calculating the distance and realizing they were too far away.

"I don't think he's following us," he told her. "I think we got away."

She nodded but didn't let off the accelerator. "I'm not stopping to find out."

Marcus's heart was still racing from what had just transpired, but he noticed Bethany seemed calm and self-assured. He couldn't even detect a drop of sweat on her brow. "What happened?" he asked, realizing she'd just saved his life.

"Something is going on. All the evidence we obtained from the sniper's nest was missing. Only, it wasn't just taken, the labels were missing and even the documentation in the evidence log had been changed."

That was indeed disturbing. "Someone on the inside?" But who at the police station in Little Falls, Texas, had reason enough to try to assassinate him?

"I don't think so. This has all the markings of a CIA operation."

"That doesn't make sense. You're bringing me in for interrogation."

"I'm been thinking about this, Marcus. If, as you claim, you haven't been targeted before today, I think someone must have been shadowing my investigation and followed me here to confront you. When they realized you were alive, they tried to take you out."

"But why? That doesn't make any sense."

"I don't know, but I suspect someone in the CIA doesn't want you to make it to Langley alive."

Marcus instructed Bethany to head north out of town. They'd made a clean getaway but neither of them harbored any doubt that the assailant would be back.

But, for now, they needed a safe place to regroup and evaluate their situation.

He motioned toward an upcoming road that would take them to the Martinez home. Bethany didn't argue the point or even ask where they were going. She was busy on her phone, dialing her boss and getting no answer. Marcus owed her his life. If she hadn't come back inside, he would be dead in his cell. *Thank You, God.* Finally she sighed in frustration. "Why won't he answer?"

He saw worry on her face and tried to remedy it. "Maybe he left his phone at home."

"No, Rick always has it with him. He's never been out of contact for this long."

The house lights came on as they approached. Marcus spotted Milo open the front door then step out, a shotgun at his side. He set it down when he spotted Marcus then called inside, no doubt to alert Marie of their arrival. Together, they met them at the car when Bethany parked.

"Are you sure you want to get these people involved?" she asked him. "What if the shooter shows up here?"

"They're good people and they care for me. I don't want to put them in danger but we need a place to lay low until we figure out our next move."

"We shouldn't stay long. If this guy is as highly trained as I suspect he is, he'll find us soon."

Marcus stared at the older couple who had taken him in and been like a family to him for the past few months. He didn't want to bring them any extra trouble, but he didn't know where else to turn. He hadn't realized when he'd started this journey that he would be placing people's lives—people he cared about—in danger. That didn't sit right with him.

Marie greeted him with a kiss and a hug when they got out of the car while Milo shook his hand.

"We knew it had to be a mistake," she stated. "They had to let you go."

"No, they didn't let me go. There was a shooting at the jailhouse. Bethany saved my life."

Marie looked at her and smiled. "Thank you."

"We won't stay long. We'll be gone in the morning."

"Of course you're welcome to stay here," Marie reassured her. "What should we do? Call the police?"

"No," Bethany told them. "The more people know we're here, the easier it'll be for him to find us. The best thing you can do to help is to just go on about your business. It's late and I can see we woke you. Go back to bed. We'll be gone by the morning."

They did as she suggested and reluctantly returned to their house while Marcus and Bethany entered the small garage apartment where he'd been staying. She sat across from Marcus at the small kitchen table. "Who attacked you?" she asked him, watching for a reaction.

He glanced at her, surprised by her question, then indignant that she still didn't believe him. "I don't know. How many times do I have to say it? I. Don't. Know." He kicked back the chair as he stood and strode to the sink.

He leaned into the sink and she saw the hunch of his shoulders. She wanted so much to believe him and in a way she did, but she couldn't let it go.

"You have to tell me what you've been up to, Marcus. Where have you been these past two years? Who have you been with? And why do they want you dead?"

He turned and looked at her again, anger blazing in his eyes. "Okay, I'm going to tell you the truth. Before I came to Little Falls, I spent a year working on an oil freighter. A man in the village where I was rescued was making the journey to work there and he allowed me to tag along, which was a huge deal because we would have both been killed if he'd been found with me. We trekked through Afghanistan and Iran and made our way to the Strait of Hormuz and got jobs on the freighter. The captain was paying cash for cheap labor and pocketing the difference between that and what the oil company paid. I worked for months for hardly nothing in order to save up the money to purchase a counterfeit passport to get me back into the US."

She nodded. That was the identification she'd used to track him down. She waited to hear more but he seemed finished with his story. "That's it? That's all you're giving me?"

"I don't know what you want from me, Bethany. I spent months recovering from my injuries that I suppose I sustained in the ambush. Then I was on the freighter or traveling to it. Then I was here. That's it. That's all I know."

She shook her head. "There must be something more. Was there someone on the freighter that you crossed who might come after you?"

"There was no one."

"What about the man who traveled with you? Could he be hunting you?"

"No. He left the tanker one day while we were docked. He never came back. I heard through my shipmates that he'd been killed in a knife fight when he tried to buy a drink for another man's girl. I was sad he was gone, but we weren't close friends. His father had made him let me tag along and he didn't appreciate it very much."

She looked as though she felt like banging her head against the table. "I need answers and I need them now. I just can't get past the feeling that the incident at the sheriff's office had CIA written all over it. But why would anyone there want you dead?"

He didn't know but he shared her sentiment that this was more than a random shooting. Someone had targeted him.

"Who are you calling?" Marcus asked as she dialed the number for information.

"The airport. With Rick not answering his line and this attack at the sheriff's office, we can't afford to wait for the Marshals to arrive to take us back to Langley. I'm chartering a plane to Virginia and we're getting out of here. We'll be out of town and back at the Agency before whoever is after you has had their morning coffee."

He listened to her make the arrangements and knew it was for the best. The sooner they were out of Little Falls, the sooner he might find the answers he'd been searching for.

A few hours later a car pulled into the driveway. Marcus braced himself. Was the sniper back to finish the job? He grabbed a gun as Bethany peered out the window. He heard her breathe a sigh of relief.

"It's only the sheriff."

She met Sheriff Mills at the door and invited him inside. He gave Marcus a cautious look then addressed Bethany.

"I figured you would come here. I knew he was staying with Milo and Marie. My deputy updated me on what happened at the station. We've been through it from top to bottom. In addition to the evidence being taken, all the security cameras were disabled and the phone lines cut. This looks like a professional hit." He glanced at Marcus and narrowed his eyes. "Someone went to a lot of trouble to get to you, Marcus. I thought you were just a drifter but, clearly, I was wrong. What are you in to?"

"I've told you before, Sheriff Mills, that I can't remember."

"Ah, right. The amnesia story."

"It's not a story."

The sheriff turned to Bethany. "Do you have any idea who this guy is who's after him? Is he one of yours?"

"No one in the CIA knew I was coming here or that Marcus was alive, but it does seem like an inside job."

"You want me to take him back to the station with me?"

Marcus shook his head. "I'm not going back in that jail cell. I'll be a sitting duck when he comes for me again. He's already proved he can get in and out of the station unseen." He looked at Bethany. "I've already told you I'll go with you. There's no need to lock me up."

She sighed. "He's right. It's too dangerous to return

him to the jail. We'll stay here tonight and be gone in the morning. I've already made the arrangements."

Sheriff Mills stood, his exasperation evident. "I'll post a deputy by the street. I don't mean to be rude, but we're a small town and we don't need trouble like this."

"Don't worry, Sheriff. We're hitting the road at daylight."

The lawman walked out, got into his car and left.

Bethany turned to Marcus and flashed him a warning look. "We'll leave in the morning. Don't try to run, Marcus, because I will find you."

"I'm not going anywhere."

"You'd better not try to make a fool of me again."

She walked over to the sofa and sat, but he knew she wasn't letting down her guard. He wondered when he'd ever made a fool of her before.

The closest big airport was in Dallas, a two-hour drive away, so Bethany had chartered an aircraft to meet them at the Little Falls airstrip. Since there was no coffee shop and they'd left Milo and Marie's house early, Bethany poured herself a cup of coffee from a machine that dispensed it black.

Marcus sat in the waiting area, his knee jerking anxiously. She'd seen that particular nervous tick of his before when he'd been preparing to head into a fight. She caught herself smiling at it. Then she remembered the last time she'd seen it. The night of the ambush.

"Why are you so nervous?" she asked, taking the seat beside him.

"Lots of reasons," he stated brusquely. "I'm about

to walk into CIA headquarters and I have no idea what I'm going to tell them. Also, there's some lunatic trying to murder me and I have no idea why."

She didn't care for his tone but she let it go. She'd seen him mask his fear that way before and suspected that was what was happening now. The villagers who'd helped him had planted a fear of the CIA in him and now he was about to walk right into the Agency headquarters. That had to be taking a toll on him emotionally. And he had every reason to be anxious, especially if he was trying to keep something from the CIA.

Their names were called and they walked over to the check-in. Bethany shook hands with the pilot.

"My name is Captain Williams. I'll be your pilot today. I've done preflight checks and filed our flight plan to Virginia. If you'd like to board now, we'll be on our way."

Bethany nodded and they headed outside to the tarmac. She was growing excited to be walking back into Langley with a catch like Marcus. Rick had said himself that he'd believed Bethany was chasing shadows, and she'd proven him wrong. She couldn't wait to walk back into headquarters with a win in her column. Perhaps it could finally overshadow her epic failure in Afghanistan.

At the plane, she reached for her bag and stopped, realizing it wasn't on her shoulder.

Marcus stopped, too. "What's wrong?"

"My computer bag. I must have left it in the terminal. I can't leave without it." She turned and rushed back down the stairs. Marcus followed.

She'd just reached the bottom of the steps when an explosion rocked the plane, tossing them through the air.

Bethany landed with a thud against the pavement. She felt the heat on her back and the pain that ripped through her shoulder as she landed hard. The explosion rang in her ears as her head connected with the pavement, sending pain riddling through her. She groaned and tried not to move, but she couldn't resist looking back at the plane. It was now a burning inferno.

As darkness seeped over her, she couldn't help but think that their attacker had nearly won again.

Heat burned behind him. Marcus groaned and glanced around. The plane was ablaze and debris was falling from the sky. His ears were ringing as images began to flash through his head of gunfire and the night sky alight and the roar of planes overhead. He shook his head to clear it. He spotted Bethany a few feet away and realized her jacket was on fire. He rushed to her and stamped it out. She was unconscious, but breathing.

Cradling her against him, he glanced at the plane again. They would have been inside that airplane if Bethany hadn't forgotten her computer bag. *Thank You, Lord.* He'd been watching out for them both. But what had happened? Was the explosion a simple mechanical failure…or had their sniper returned to finish what he'd started?

Bethany stirred in his arms and he stared down at her. "It's okay, Beth. I got you."

She opened her eyes and looked at him, then smiled and reached out, gently stroking his cheek. "Marcus."

She whispered his name then leaned up and kissed him softly on the lips.

He was stunned, unable to move or speak. But when she closed her eyes and fell back against him, he knew she hadn't been fully aware of her actions. However, he was certain of one thing. She'd been glad to see him and she'd kissed him like she'd done it a million times before.

He glanced around. People were running from the terminal with fire extinguishers and emergency tools. Someone knelt beside them.

"Are you hurt?"

"I'm fine, but I think she hit her head."

"The paramedics are on the way. Keep her still until they get here." The first responder ran off to help with the fire.

Marcus stayed with Bethany until they arrived then reluctantly moved aside. She still had not regained consciousness and that worried him. They'd both been sent flying by the impact of the blast. Had she suffered a concussion when she'd landed?

One of the paramedics turned to him. "Sir, we need to treat you, too."

"I'm fine," he said. "Concentrate on her."

"My partner is taking care of the lady. Please, you have a bad cut on your head."

He reached up and touched his temple. His hand came back bloody. He hadn't even noticed. Finally he conceded and allowed the woman to treat the few scrapes and cuts he'd sustained. He had been fortunate he hadn't been hurt worse. No, he thought. Not fortunate. God had been looking out for him again, just as He had during his trek from Afghanistan back to the US. This was just one more example of how the good Lord continued to shield Marcus.

He spotted the sheriff and hurried over to him. "Sheriff, do we know what caused this yet?"

Sheriff Mills turned to him then nodded. "What are you doing here?" He glanced around. "Where's Agent Bryant?"

"This was our plane. Bethany chartered it to go to Virginia. She was injured in the blast. The paramedics are with her now. Do we know what happened?"

"You tell me. You were here."

Marcus rubbed a hand over his face. "We were getting on the plane when Bethany realized she'd left her computer in the terminal. We were going back for it. That's when the explosion occurred. Do we know yet what caused it?"

"We're just beginning our investigation, but I'd advise you not to leave town. I'll have questions for both you and Agent Bryant."

Marcus nodded and looked back, noticing they were loading Bethany into an ambulance. "I'm going to ride to the hospital with her."

"Fine. Wait for me there."

Marcus hurried over and hopped into the ambulance for the ride to the hospital.

Pain ripped through Bethany's head and pulled her back to consciousness. She felt something soft against her skin and realized she was in a bed before she even opened her eyes. The room was dimly lit, though a faint light streaming in from behind the closed curtains was enough for her to see with. She tried to pull her hand to her aching head but found her motion limited by IV tubes. She was in a hospital but she couldn't readily remember why.

Then it all came back to her—the airport, returning for her bag, the explosion.

Marcus!

She jerked awake and spotted him stretched out in the chair by the bed. Relief rushed through her that he was okay. Then amazement. Why had he stuck around? He'd had the perfect opportunity to escape but hadn't. He was sleeping soundly but she noticed the bandages on his head and neck. He'd been hurt in the explosion, but how badly?

He stirred, as if realizing she was watching him, opened his eyes and gave her a lazy grin. "You're awake. How do you feel?"

"You're here?"

"Of course. I'm not going anywhere." He noticed her surprise and sat up. "I told you, Bethany, I want answers. I'm not going to run at my first opportunity to find them."

He'd said he wanted answers, but that was before the shootings, the altercations and now this. What lengths would these people go to, to keep him from knowing the truth? "Even if someone will resort to blowing up an airplane to keep you from getting those answers?"

He pressed his lips together and gave her a pointed look. "Yeah, even then. I won't be frightened away from discovering the truth." He jumped to his feet and ran an annoyed hand through his hair "In fact, the more they try to keep me silent, the more I want to know. What kind of people was I involved with that will shoot into diners or blow up planes?"

"How long have I been here?"

"Nine hours. You're not badly hurt but you did hit your head and suffer some minor cuts and burns."

She motioned toward his bandages. "And you?"

"The same."

A sense of relief flowed through her. They'd escaped death once again. "We were fortunate."

"No," he said quickly, locking eyes with her determinedly. "Fortune had nothing to do with it. God was watching out for us both today."

Bethany sighed. If he wanted to believe that, fine, but she wasn't going to buy into that kind of thinking. God had left her a long time ago. She pushed back the blanket covering her and slid her feet to the floor.

"What are you doing?" he asked.

"Getting dressed." She pulled at the tape securing her IV to her hand. Struggling to remove it, she couldn't help thinking they must have used an entire roll.

He moved to her bedside. "You shouldn't get up. The doctor said you have a slight concussion."

That explained the ache in her head but she wasn't going to allow a little thing like a head injury to stop her. "I'm fine," she said, pushing to her feet. The room quickly began to spin and she clutched the bed for support.

"You're in no condition to get up," he insisted.

"I need to talk to the authorities to find out the status of the investigation. Who's in charge of it?"

"Sheriff Mills. He said he would stop by later once you were awake."

"Well, I'm awake now." And she wasn't going to speak with the sheriff while wearing a hospital gown. "Where are my clothes?"

Marcus motioned at a cabinet and she walked toward it. Pulling out her clothes, she went into the bathroom to change, ignoring every pound in her head and every ache in her muscles.

She dressed quickly, opened the door and stepped out, stumbling over her feet and falling right into Marcus's arms. He caught her, sweeping her close in his strong embrace.

She swallowed hard as she stared into his soft green eyes and remembered the many months she had ached for his embrace when she'd thought he was dead. Her heart hammered so hard in her chest that it drowned out the pain in her head and body. She struggled to even catch her breath when she was this close to him.

She pushed back from him, trying to find some semblance of her dignity. She couldn't deny her attraction to him, but she'd sworn she would not allow herself to fall prey to his cunning again. "I'm fine," she said, her voice unsteady. He seemed so stable and so concerned and determined. But was it all just an act? She couldn't take the risk.

"We…we need to go see Sheriff Mills and find out what's going on with the investigation."

The hospital door opened and the sheriff walked in. "I guess I've got good timing, don't I?"

She took another step away from Marcus and felt her face redden as if the sheriff had just caught them in a compromising position. She also felt a rush of relief that at least he hadn't walked in when she was in his arms. "Sheriff, I was just on my way to speak with you." She forced her voice to a normal tone. "Do you know yet what caused the explosion?"

"We do. That's why I'm here. The fire marshal discovered the remains of a bomb."

Her heart fell. "A *bomb*? Really?" She had been hoping this was a simple case of an accidental explosion, a fuel leak or an electrical fire. She sighed, seeing the same resignation on Marcus's face that she felt.

The sheriff continued. "The pilot didn't make it out, but thankfully you two did."

She nodded. "Yes, I left my bag in the terminal. We turned around to go back for it. If we hadn't, we would have both been on the plane when the bomb detonated."

She felt saddened for the loss of the pilot and wondered if he had a family who would miss him. "Before he boarded, the pilot stated that he'd done his preflight checks. How did he miss a bomb?"

"It was hidden under the fuselage. He probably wouldn't have seen it when he checked the plane. The preliminary results on the explosive indicate that it was homemade and was likely placed on a timer set to detonate at a certain time."

"That's why it still went off even though we'd disembarked the plane," Marcus stated. "He had no way to stop it."

She sighed. "And being homemade means the perp used whatever he could find locally to make it."

The sheriff nodded. "We've already started calling local hardware and warehouse stores to follow up on anyone who might have purchased the ingredients we've identified as part of the bomb. The manifest listed only two passengers on this flight. The two of you." He pointed to each of them.

"Yes, that's true," she explained. "I chartered the plane last night to return us to Langley."

"Who knew you were chartering this plane today?"

Bethany's forehead crinkled as she tried to think back. She hadn't told anyone about her plans and in fact had made them late last night. "Anyone from the airport could have had knowledge. Other than that, I don't know."

Sheriff Mills turned his gaze to Marcus, who shook his head.

"I didn't tell anyone. Milo and Marie knew we were leaving, but I didn't go into details about where or how."

"Our preliminary investigation hasn't turned up anything about the pilot that might indicate he was into something that could have gotten him killed. Right now we're acting on the assumption that one or both of you were the targets."

It seemed a logical conclusion given the sniper on the roof and the shoot-out at the jail. "Someone doesn't want us returning to Langley," she said, the idea truly beginning to take hold in her mind.

"It's more than that," Marcus retorted, locking eyes with Bethany. "Someone doesn't want me to make it out of town alive."

She was beginning to suspect he was right. But who?

Bethany swept a hand through her hair. "I need to update my supervisor about all that's happened."

The sheriff cleared his throat. "There's just one more thing. Don't leave town. I might have further questions for the two of you."

"I'll go back to Milo and Marie's tonight," Marcus said. "I'm sure they'll want to keep Bethany here overnight for observation."

"I'm not staying here," she insisted. "I'll go back to the house with you."

Sheriff Mills nodded. "I'll be in touch," he said before turning and walking out.

Marcus stood. "I'll give you some privacy so you can phone your boss."

Her knee-jerk response was to stop him and not let him out of her sight, but she knew now that that was unnecessary. He'd had his chance to leave and he hadn't. He'd stayed with her, even camped out in her hospital room to make certain she was okay after the explosion. His behavior seemed to belie the traitor she believed him to be. Did that mean his claims of amnesia were true and he really was searching for answers about who he was? And if that was the case, what would he do when he discovered he was a bad guy?

But Marcus and bad guy were two concepts she was having a hard time reconciling. It seemed to fly in the face of who he was or who she'd thought he was. In fact, until the moment she'd seen him walking toward her at Milo's diner, she hadn't truly believed it possible he was alive.

She dug through her bag, found her cell phone, thankfully undamaged by the day's events, and dialed Rick's number. He hadn't answered last night and she briefly wondered if he would now, but to her relief he answered on the first ring.

"Rick, where have you been? I've been trying to reach you."

"Sorry, kid. I had an emergency meeting that couldn't be stopped. How's our soldier? I haven't had an opportunity to follow up with the Marshals."

"We couldn't wait on the Marshals," Bethany told him then explained all that had happened since they had last spoken. "I'm worried about our safety. Someone doesn't want Marcus to return to Langley and spill what he knows."

Rick's tone grew serious. "I'm going to fill you in on something most people don't know." She heard him get up from his desk, walk across his office and close his door.

"Uh-oh. Sounds ominous."

"The Agency has been investigating the possibility of a rogue agent recruiting soldiers for the enemy. It's apparently been happening for a while but no one has been able to gather any evidence. Right now, it's just a rumor, but it's a reputable rumor."

"You think Marcus is one of those soldiers who got recruited?"

"It's possible, isn't it?"

She couldn't deny it was a possibility. Yet, again, it seemed to go against everything he was.

"Obviously, Marcus knows who's after him."

"He's sticking to his amnesia story. He still claims he doesn't remember."

"I don't know what kind of game he's playing, but I suspect once we get him here, he'll offer what he knows for some kind of deal. I've already informed the legal department. He'll probably get a plea bargain if he comes clean. If we have a traitor in our midst, we need to know who it is and soon."

Bethany shuddered at the thought that someone in the CIA could be working against them. A traitor in plain sight. And Marcus held the key to identifying him. "How should I proceed?"

"You have to get him to Langley for questioning, but don't go through regular channels or involve other agencies. I'll put the word out that you're on leave and then you can make arrangements to quietly bring him in. We need to have answers about where he's been and what he's been doing. More importantly, if he can identify the agent who recruited him, we can finally bring that guy to justice."

"I'll do my best," she said then ended the call.

Bethany suddenly felt the weight of the responsibility Rick had just placed on her shoulders.

She'd been operating alone on finding Marcus for two years and had been looking forward to having the weight of the Agency behind her now. Bethany sighed. She was on her own again in bringing Marcus in.

She closed her eyes and wished for someone to depend on. Once upon a time, she would have turned to God for strength and reassurance, but her relationship with the Almighty wasn't quite what it used to be. Losing Marcus and then learning she'd been betrayed by him had damaged her ability to trust, and that included God. He could have warned her, showed her signs that Marcus could not be trusted, or at least have guarded her heart from falling for him. But He hadn't. He'd allowed her to fall head over heels and suffer because of it.

That, she could not forgive.

FOUR

Marcus drove back to his apartment at Milo and Marie's house. He looked at Bethany in the passenger's seat. She should have stayed at the hospital, but she'd stubbornly refused. They'd had a close call but God had truly been watching out for them. He just wished he knew who was after him and why.

Milo greeted them at the door and welcomed them back. Marcus hadn't told them what had happened with the airplane but it was a small town and he was certain they'd heard by now. Before they went inside, he pulled Milo aside to make certain they were still invited to stay there.

"You know you're always welcome here, son."

"I don't want to put you and Marie out. We just need a safe place to stay for another night."

"Stay," Milo assured him. "We take care of our own around here."

He thanked his friend then walked back to the SUV and found Bethany pulling out a large box from the back.

"What are those?" Marcus asked, reaching to help her.

"Oh, this? This is your life, Marcus. Every file, mention and scrap of paper I've gathered tracking your movements from Afghanistan to here. You and I are going to dig through it. Maybe you'll see something I missed. I think we can both agree that whoever is after you, I led them here. They've been following my search for you."

He glanced at her, surprised. "Someone knew I was alive. That's who my caretakers who nursed me back to health were so afraid of."

She nodded. "And if they're CIA, the villagers who hid you risked their lives to do so. The Afghani people are on the front lines, dealing with operatives and soldiers every day. If they were hiding you instead of handing you over to the army, either they were looking for an opportunity to cash in or they were just plain scared of whoever was after you."

Marcus didn't like the scenario she was painting. He was wanted by the government and now, apparently, by some dark force inside the CIA, as well. What on earth had he done to elicit such animosity?

He carried the box inside and placed it on the table. He couldn't wait to search through the files, but first he needed to know something.

"Tell me about that night, the night of the ambush."

"Marcus, I don't think now—"

"This may very well be the last moment I have to hear it before someone bursts through that door to kill me. What happened that night?"

She sighed, resigned, and slowly slid into a chair. "We had what we thought was credible intel that a high-powered official in the Taliban was hiding out in a compound. Your ranger team was called in to act as point for an assault. It was a coordinated operation that took days of planning and preparation. However, once we arrived, we realized our intel was wrong."

"Wrong? How so?"

"The cars were out of place and the livestock had been moved. When your team arrived, armed men began shooting. Delta charged in to help and many of them died, too. All in all, only six members of your team survived that night. It was later determined that the Afghani man I recruited as a translator betrayed us." She swallowed hard. "We were unable to locate him after the ambush. However, four months later, I read a cable stating he'd been found dead, assassinated by the Taliban. That was when I began to suspect something greater had occurred that night than the official reports stated."

"But what happened to me?"

"I don't know, Marcus. We don't have an official report to track you that night. However, one of your teammates, Garrett Lewis, reported seeing you lying on the ground and said you weren't moving. He was convinced you were dead and turned to help one of the other rangers who was hurt, Levi Thompson." Hitching in a breath, she met his gaze. "I know this man, Marcus. I met Garrett before the ambush and the two of you were close friends. He wouldn't have left if there'd been doubt that you were alive. I heard he didn't handle it well when they were unable to recover your body."

"Garrett Lewis? Levi Thompson?"

Her blue eyes lit up. "Are those names ringing any bells?"

He hated to dash the spark he'd seen there, but he shook his head. The names were unfamiliar to him. "None."

She dug through the boxes, pulled out a photo of his squad and handed it to him. "This was taken two days before the ambush."

He took the photo and saw that it was a team picture. Men in khaki uniforms and hats, holding guns. He scanned the faces, stunned when he spotted his own. It was like seeing someone who looked just like him. However, that Marcus Allen was nothing but a mystery to him.

She moved to sit beside him, scanning the photo before pointing out the surviving rangers. She rattled off their names—Josh Adams, Garrett Lewis, Levi Thompson, Matt Ross, Blake Michaels, Colton Blackwell—but all he heard was the beating of his heart as the sweet scent of her skin wafted into his nostrils. Nothing about the ambush or his teammates seemed familiar…but she did. She was the first familiar thing he'd discovered in two years.

Bethany glanced up at him and her eyes widened, probably at the spark of attraction he was sure blanketed his face. The familiar, wide blue eyes and graceful curve of her round face called to him. He reached out and stroked her jaw, moving down to her lips. She didn't pull away. At least, not at first. Her head bobbed backward and her breathing heightened. He wanted to kiss her, just as he had a hundred times before in his dreams. It was her he'd been remembering. He'd never been more certain of anything in his life.

Suddenly she tensed, pushed his hand away and stood, putting some distance between them.

"No, I can't," she said, but her voice was hoarse with emotion. He knew she recognized the attraction between them and she was just as moved by it as he was.

She turned back to the files on the table. "I should probably go over the other details I uncovered that made me realize you hadn't died that night."

Marcus propped his hands on the table and stared at her. He wasn't interested in facts and details, not when the truth was standing right in front of him and evading his questions.

"Tell me about us, Bethany."

She seemed flustered, which surprised him. He wouldn't have thought anything could unnerve her. "I don't know what you're talking about."

He waved his hand over the table full of file folders. "None of this, these papers and facts and details, have given me the slightest bit of familiarity that I just felt and *have felt* since the moment I laid eyes on you." He moved toward her. "Please, Bethany. I just want to know something about my life. Who are you? Who are you to me?"

She could have turned and told him she was his wife, lover, longtime girlfriend, and he wouldn't have batted an eye. That was how strongly he felt he knew her. But she didn't say any of those things.

"I'm nothing to you, Marcus."

He clenched his jaw and gave her a disbelieving look. "I know that's not true."

"You want the truth, Marcus? Then I will lay it out for you…

"We met two weeks before the ambush, when I arrived at the base to work on the logistics of the operation. When the teams weren't actively on a mission, they often acted as bodyguards for CIA field agents. You were assigned to my protection detail, which meant you had to drive me around." She snickered softly. "You were so mad at first. You hated that assignment. But, after a couple of days and a lot of time spent together, you changed. You made me laugh. I liked that because my work was always so serious." She folded her arms at her waist as her voice cracked. "Given enough time, I thought we could have had something real between us, but our time just ran out." She started packing up files and he could see that wasn't the entire story.

"What else?"

"You made me care for you, Marcus, and then you were gone. I was so angry at you for that and I was angry that God would allow it to happen and then snatch you away. However, all that changed when I began to suspect you weren't dead." She released a sharp breath. "There were rumors of an American being hidden inside an Afghani village. They couldn't be substantiated, so there wasn't an official investigation, but I knew it was you."

"But how could you be so sure?" he demanded softly.

She shrugged. "The pieces just seemed to fit. They never found your body and then these rumors surfaced.

That's when I knew you had to be alive. But then, as the months passed and you never contacted anyone, or me, I began to suspect something was awry with your disappearance. I told myself if you didn't die that night then you'd planned to leave. You'd planned to make me fall for you and then leave me."

A look of shock and disbelief shadowed his face as she continued.

"I started questioning everything. Why would you do that? Did I have something or know something that you needed from me? And, most importantly, did you get it? You did more than run out on me, Marcus. You made me question my ability as an analyst. I couldn't even trust my own judgment after that night." Her voice cracked and she swallowed back a sob. "I tried twice to go back out into the field, but I just couldn't, so I applied for a desk job. It's lower risk and, given my coworkers, there's very little chance of me getting my heart broken."

"I'm sorry I hurt you, Bethany, but I have a hard time believing it was by design. Every time I try to see my past, all I can see is you."

"It doesn't matter anymore, does it?"

"It might," he said gruffly.

"I'll never let my guard down that way again. It hurt too much. Besides, I don't think I could ever trust you, Marcus. I would always be waiting for the other boot to drop."

Her words sounded so final and so full of pain. He hated that he'd hurt her, but could she really hold him responsible for something he didn't remember doing?

A wave of frustration swept through him. He could not even defend himself because he did not know the truth. Had he been using her to gather information? His gut told him no. His attraction to Bethany was too real, too intense, to have been faked.

He loaded up the rest of the files and replaced the top on the box. She was right. It didn't matter. He couldn't find the answers she needed until he uncovered his own answers. Maybe he had hurt her on purpose. Maybe he had been acting on orders. Whatever the deal, he needed to find out.

He shuddered, realizing he might discover something worse—that he wasn't worthy of someone like Bethany.

No matter what, he had to find out.

"Bethany, you have to give me some time to regain my memories. I can't walk back into CIA headquarters without knowing the truth about myself. They'll railroad me. I think it's been proved that someone in the CIA doesn't want me to talk. How do I even know who I can trust if I have no clue what's going on?"

His words didn't surprise her, but she couldn't agree to his request. "Don't ask me to do that, Marcus. I have a job to do."

"And you'll be doing your job…just a little delayed. I'm not asking you to let me go. I only want an opportunity to find out for myself what happened that night."

Still, she hesitated. She was supposed to bring him in.

"Your boss told you to bring me in. You'll still do so. We'll just make a few detours along the way."

She had to admit she, too, wanted to know the truth before they walked into CIA headquarters. Was he right that he would be made a scapegoat? She'd heard the rumors about how the Agency operated. Was it possible he might disappear and she would never know the truth? There was so much uncertainty right now, but he *was* right about one thing: she didn't know who she could trust at the Agency.

She wanted to believe she could count on Rick, but he'd been insistent that she not mention her plans to anyone. Did that mean there were people around him who didn't have his back?

Once again, she was torn between her loyalty to Marcus and her sense of duty to the CIA. Her gut told her that she could trust Marcus, but she'd been burned by him before.

"Let's go," she said, reaching for her purse.

"Where are we going?"

"Back to the hospital."

He jumped up. "Are you all right? Do you need me to call for an ambulance?"

"It's not for me. It's for you."

They made the drive back to the hospital and tracked down the doctor who had reluctantly given Bethany her discharge papers.

He looked concerned when he spotted them approaching.

"Agent Bryant. You've returned. Are you having any problems?"

She didn't need to go over her medial issues with

him. Instead she got right to the point. "What do you know about amnesia, Dr. Wayne?"

He glanced at her, concerned. "Are you suffering with memory loss?"

"It's not me." She looked at Marcus, who was standing behind her, and Dr. Wayne nodded knowingly.

"It's okay, Doc," Marcus said and then glanced at Bethany. "One of the first things Marie insisted on when I arrived in town was that I see a doctor about my memory loss. Dr. Wayne did an MRI and determined there was no damage to my frontal lobe."

Bethany shook her head, stunned that he'd not mentioned this. "What does that mean?"

Dr. Wayne responded. "One of the most common forms of amnesia is retrograde amnesia, basically the loss of past memories. It can be due to either traumatic brain injury or a traumatic event that results in memories being repressed to protect the mind. We've already ruled out a physical cause for his amnesia, which means there is a good likelihood that he can retrieve those memories in time."

Bethany's heart fell. No physical reason to believe he was suffering amnesia. No, that would have made her decision to trust him too easy. She felt her face redden. Had she really been rooting for brain damage? "So how does he do that?"

"The study of the brain and especially memory is not an exact science. There's still a lot we don't know about the mind and its functions. He needs to immerse himself in things that are familiar. I told him this before, but, of course, he didn't know anything that was familiar. Now that you can provide his true identity, you might be able to make it happen. Unfortunately, there are no guarantees. If you haven't recovered them by now, you may never."

Marcus looked to her. Confusion filled his expression and she was certain he was wondering what she would do if his memories never returned. There was no question in her mind. She would do what she had to do—return him to Langley to face his crimes. And what would they do to him when he couldn't—or wouldn't—tell them who he'd been working for?

Her heart broke thinking about what he might suffer for his actions but her own mind was still spinning in confusion. Why wouldn't he run if he knew what he was facing once they returned to Langley? And if he did know who was after him, why would he risk not returning immediately?

Bethany sighed, facing the truth she'd been fighting for the past twenty-four hours. She believed him when he said he couldn't remember. She had believed him since the first moment she'd seen him walking toward her without a shred of recognition on his face.

It was the only hope she had to cling to that maybe he wasn't the monster she'd spent the past two years convincing herself he was.

Marcus drove as they returned to his apartment. Bethany was silent beside him and he could see she was wrestling with herself about what to do. He wondered if her silent struggle was obvious to everyone else, but something about it seemed familiar to him, as if he'd seen this expression on her face before.

"Are you sure you're ready for this?" she asked him quietly, breaking the silence in the SUV.

"Ready for what?"

"What if we go through all this, Marcus, only to discover that it's all true? That you're a traitor and that you used me to gather information."

He tightened his grip on the steering wheel. That thought haunted his every waking moment, but he would not allow it to stop him from finding out the truth. "At least I would know for sure. If I'm going to prison, I want to at least know what I did to belong there."

He turned into the driveway that led to his garage apartment and stopped in front of the door.

Bethany turned and stared up at him, but he couldn't read her expression so her words surprised him. "I'll give you three days to discover the truth, but you have to make me a promise, Marcus. Once those three days are over, you'll return with me to Langley regardless of what you find out."

He breathed a sigh of relief. "Yes, I promise," he said. He'd given his word to her that he would return with her and he had no intention of reneging on that promise, but this extra time might provide him answers he'd been seeking. He'd already discovered more about himself in the past two days than in the past two years. Three days wasn't a lot, but it might be crucial to uncovering what he needed to know about his past.

"Fine. I'll follow your lead, but we need to leave this

place tonight. It won't take the sniper long to figure out where we are. I would suggest we go now, except that I need a few hours of sleep. Whoever is after us won't stop until you're dead. I don't want to make it easy for him to complete his mission."

Marcus nodded. He agreed that leaving was for the best. He loved Milo and Marie. They'd been like a family to him when he'd had no one, but he wasn't willing to put them at risk any more than he already had. "I'll be ready."

They went inside and she retired to the bedroom. Marcus couldn't sleep so he spent the next few hours poring over the files she had collected. So far, nothing was jumping out at him. Bethany had been thorough in her work and doggedly persistent. He smiled, liking that she hadn't given up.

But had she given up on him already?

A knock on the door that connected his little apartment with Milo and Marie's home caught his attention. Marcus opened the door and saw Milo standing there, still wearing his bathrobe and slippers. He glanced at the clock, realizing it was just pushing 3:00 a.m.

"I saw your light," Milo stated. "Having trouble sleeping?" he asked.

Marcus nodded. "You could say that."

Milo poured himself a mug of coffee from the pot Marcus had made earlier. He joined Marcus at the table and flipped through a couple of folders. "Finding anything?"

"No, nothing. These files may as well be talking

about someone else. I waited for so long to find out who I am and now that I know, he's like a stranger to me."

He pushed the files away as he lowered himself into a chair. "This isn't you, Marcus."

"It's my service files."

"Maybe this is who you used to be, but it's not you anymore. You've been through too much."

He took a sip from his mug. "That's what I'm afraid of. Bethany told me some things about myself, things she knew about me, and I didn't like them too much. If they're true…let's just say I'm not looking forward to discovering I'm some kind of villain."

"Even if you were, who cares?"

"The federal government for one. I might be a deserter and a traitor."

"I can't believe that. It's not who you are. I don't believe people change that much. What you've been through, your ordeal, the gunshots and nearly dying… Those kinds of things bring out the real character of a person and they've only brought out the good in you."

"Maybe, but the evidence…"

Milo tossed a folder back into the box. "This paperwork isn't going to tell you who you are, Marcus. You need to reconnect with yourself, like the way you have with Bethany. When you're with her, your memories seem sharper. Your true colors shine through."

Marcus saw where the older man's line of thinking was going and grabbed hold of one thought. "You're right. I had more of a reaction after a few minutes with Bethany than I have the whole four hours I've been pouring through these files. I need to connect with the people who knew me."

He dug through and found his service folder, then flipped it open to reveal his home address and next of kin. "I have a mother and a sister living in Waco. And if I had any personal items, the army would have shipped them to them." There was no photo of his mother or sister in his file and, to his frustration, he couldn't conjure up one image of them. On a whim, he entered the address into the GPS on his phone and realized they lived only a three-hour drive away.

It was time he let his family know he was still alive.

"That's a good place to start. At the beginning." Milo stood. "Don't leave without saying goodbye, son. Marie will be sore if you do and I'll have to listen to her yacking." He gave Marcus a smile that told him the man cared deeply for his wife.

Marcus smiled back. He'd loved spending time with these two and watching how much they respected and appreciated one another. For him, they were a perfect example of what a godly marriage should be and he'd prayed one day he'd fine something similar.

He started to assure Milo they wouldn't be leaving until morning since Bethany was asleep in the bedroom, but a noise outside stopped him. He held up a hand to quiet Milo and heard the rustling of movement through the window.

Marcus dropped the box and picked up his gun. "Someone's outside." He rushed to the window and peeked through the curtain. A light shone in the distance and he spotted the telltale red laser of a scope searching for its target.

Bethany appeared in the doorway, now fully awake and on alert, her weapon drawn, having obviously heard the movement or seen the laser scope. "He's here. He found us."

Milo hurried through the door to his home then re-appeared with his shotgun.

"That won't be necessary," Marcus told him. "He's not after you. Get Marie and go down into the base-ment and stay there."

"I can't leave you two to fight off this guy," Milo insisted.

"We have Bethany's SUV packed and ready to go. He'll follow us."

Milo looked like he was about to argue the point, and Marcus was just as determined that his friend wasn't going to get involved in this fight, when a bullet ripped through the window, shattering the glass. Marcus hit the ground hard and the bullet whizzed past him. It slammed into Milo's chest.

"No!" Marcus shouted, anger pulsing through him as Milo slid to the floor.

He heard a woman scream then saw Marie appear in the doorway, having obviously seen her husband fall from the other side of the door. "Get down," Mar-cus hollered at her, but a moment later, another bullet whizzed through the window and ended her cries. She slumped over her husband and there was no doubt in Marcus's mind that neither would be getting up again.

Shock, grief and anger swept through Marcus. This

hadn't had to happen. They shouldn't have had to die. They were innocent of everything but trying to help him.

Bethany touched his arm and only then did he realize she was shouting at him. He hadn't heard her over the loud roar of his own rage sounding in his ears.

"We have to get out of here," she said. "He's got us pinned down."

But Marcus felt reason flow right out of him. He wasn't running away. The enemy was in front of him and had taken two people that he cared about. He would make him pay.

He grabbed Milo's shotgun and spun, firing through the window toward the direction from where he'd heard the shot.

Silence filled the night and for a moment Marcus thought he'd hit the sniper. Then he heard a click and a whir that he immediately knew spelled trouble.

He grabbed Bethany's arm. "Let's get out of here," he said, running through the door and into the main house as the whistle of a rocket-propelled grenade heading their way grew louder. The RPG hit the house and the ensuing explosion shook the ground, sending them both flying. Marcus hit a wall with a thud and slid to the floor. His ears were ringing and smoke filled the room as he frantically searched for Bethany. He found her on the floor, covered by the coffee table and a slew of books.

"Are you hurt?" he asked hoarsely as he dug her out.

"I'm fine," she answered, coughing at the smoke

filling the room. She dug through the rubble and re-trieved her gun.

"The garage," he said, motioning her toward the back of the house.

She nodded and followed him, limping slightly on her left foot.

A rush of thankfulness spread through him when he kicked open the door to the garage and saw Milo's truck undamaged by the explosion on the other side of the house. He grabbed the keys Milo kept by the back door, helped Bethany in then climbed inside and started the truck. He hit the garage opener but nothing happened; the power was out from the explosion. That didn't matter. They were getting out of this place even if that meant he had to ram the garage door off its rails.

Bethany checked her weapon. "I'll give us some cover fire."

He nodded. Bracing himself for the next few mo-ments, he whispered a quick prayer for their safety and also for Milo and Marie, before jamming the accelerator to the floor and flying out of the garage, taking down the door with the pickup.

The shots started coming from near the apartment and Marcus realized the shooter had come looking to finish them off. He jammed the truck into Drive and took off as Bethany leaned out the window and returned fire until they were out of range.

He stared at the house in the rearview mirror. The roof had collapsed and flames were licking at the walls that remained standing, bursting forth into the still, dark sky through various openings. The air in the truck smelled burnt and he realized they were both covered in the smoky stench. He looked at Bethany. Blood was trickling down her face from a gash on her forehead and she had been limping on her ankle, but he didn't think she was seriously injured. Neither was he. They'd both made it out intact once again.

He looked back into the mirror and a pang of agony churned through him as he remembered not everyone had made it out. He drove for several miles until he was certain they weren't being followed. Pulling the truck over to the side of the road, he stopped.

"What are we doing?" Bethany asked as he got out. Without answering, he opened the toolbox on the back of the truck. He knew Milo had kept a first-aid kit there and he quickly found it. Bethany was bleeding and that wound needed to be attended to. He opened her door and riffled through the kit until he located a roll of gauze. Tearing off a piece, he leaned down and gently dabbed her head with it.

She winced then took it from him. "I can do it."

He nodded. "Are you hurt anywhere else?" He focused on her ankle. "You were limping before," he said, running his hand down her leg and pulling it to him. He raised her jeans-clad leg and saw that her ankle was bruised and swollen. But there were no bones sticking out, which was good, and she had been able to put some weight on it back there.

"It's a little tender," she admitted. He pressed his fingers around the swollen part, finding a spot that made her gasp in pain. "Okay, more than a little."

He cracked open an ice pack and placed it on her ankle. "This might help."

"Thank you," she said, shivering when his hand brushed the smooth skin just above her injury. He glanced up and saw compassion shining in her eyes.

"I'm sorry about your friends," she said softly. "They seemed to be very nice people and it was obvious they cared for you."

His clenched his jaw at the memory of seeing first Milo and then Marie fall in front of them. He'd watched the light slip from their faces and, although he knew they were both in a much better place, his heart broke that they'd had to suffer such an indignity as being shot down in their own home.

He nodded and, when he spoke, his voice was just as raw and hoarse as his heart felt. "They were. They didn't deserve to die." He tossed the first-aid kit onto the seat then walked back around the truck and climbed inside. "It's nearly daylight. We should get some food then find a place to rest for a while. We've got a long drive ahead of us."

She sat up, curious. "What drive? What are you talking about? Where are we going?"

"You gave me three days to find answers, remember? Well, I'm not going to sit around answering Sheriff Mills' questions during that time. I'm going to find the truth on my own."

"But all my files are back at the house, probably destroyed. How do you even know where to go?"

"I was looking at my service file when the sniper attacked. I remember the address."

"Whose address? Where are we going, Marcus?"

Milo had advised him to start his search at the beginning and that was exactly what he was going to do. "My family lives in Waco. I'm going home."

FIVE

A hot shower was just what she'd needed to soothe her sore muscles. She hadn't realized when she'd started her search for Marcus that finding him would place her in the battle zone.

But then again she hadn't honestly believed she would find him alive. The past eighteen months she'd spent searching for him and chasing down leads, she'd never truly been convinced she would find a living, breathing person. But the hunt had been what had kept her going when she'd wanted to give up on living and wondering how she could go on without Marcus, despite their brief time together. Even her family had noticed the way she'd changed. She recalled her sister's words to her at a family dinner.

It's time to move on, Lisa had told her. *He's gone. It's time to get on with your life.*

But Bethany had been stuck in the eternal question of why this had happened. It all seemed like a cruel joke perpetrated against her by the Almighty for His own entertainment. And her family's strained attempts to pacify her with Christian rhetoric like "God uses all things for His purpose" did little but turn her heart away from the Lord.

She stepped outside her hotel room and tapped on Marcus's door, opening it and walking inside when he responded to do so. He was sitting on one of the double beds, his boots on the floor beside him and a book open in his lap. She moved closer and saw that it was a Gideon Bible he'd obviously taken from the hotel nightstand. She shook her head as she glanced over it. His Bible had been left in the jail cell the night of the shooting. She'd seen for herself how intensely it had been studied. It shouldn't surprise her that he was seeking comfort from its words, but it did. After all they'd been through, it baffled her how Marcus would have such faith.

He doesn't remember, she reminded herself. He doesn't know the full extent of what God had taken from them both. It was the only way she could wrap her head around it.

She peeked out the curtain into the hotel parking lot. Everything looked normal and she didn't see any suspicious activity, but she knew from experience that just because she didn't see signs of danger didn't mean it wasn't present.

"Relax," Marcus told her. "We took precautions. We checked in under assumed names, made sure no one was following us, and I parked the truck where it can't be seen from the street. We'll be safe here tonight."

Yes, they'd covered all bases, but she was still on edge.

"Feel better?" he asked, referring to her shower.

She nodded and curled up in a chair opposite him. "Much better." She motioned at the Bible on the bed. "And you?"

He sighed. "Trying to. It's not always easy to remember God is on my side. Some days, like today, it seems He's not."

She couldn't argue with his reasoning. She hadn't seen much evidence that God was around, either.

He picked up the Bible and stared at it. "I just have to remember it may not always be obvious, but God is always here with me no matter what I face. When I forget, it helps to seek His promises. Exodus 14:14. 'The Lord will fight for you. You need only to be still.'"

She rolled her eyes. "If we'd remained still tonight, we would both be dead. Besides, you're a soldier, Marcus. You were trained to take action, not sit around waiting on someone else to fight your battles."

"When I was traveling back to the US, even then I was aware of a higher power that was watching out for me, guiding me, keeping me safe from harm. My life in His hands. I have no idea what my faith looked like before I awoke in that village in Afghanistan. Was I a believer? Or was I hostile toward God back then? I do know for certain that I wouldn't be here today without the intervention of the Almighty God." Exhaling roughly, he turned to look at Bethany. "Do you know I traveled across the entire country of Iran with no identification?"

Her eyes widened in shock. "No... I had no idea."

"If I'd been stopped or captured, I would surely have been killed, but I wasn't. I made it through without a single incident that threatened my life." His voice cracked with emotion as he continued. "He guided me then and He brought me safely back to the US…and now He's taking me home. I'm going to see my family again. If that's not proof of God's existence, then I don't know what is."

Bethany stared at him. Had she ever felt such a connection to God before? She couldn't remember if she had. Her family had been in church every Sunday for as far back as she knew, but she couldn't recall even one time she'd felt God's presence the way Marcus had during his journey.

She did not bother telling him that he had never seemed particularly religious to her before the ambush. That probably wasn't what he wanted to hear and she really couldn't say for sure that it was a true statement. Perhaps he'd been very religious and she hadn't gotten to know that part of him. She might have discovered it if they'd had the time to get to know one another. She grimaced at that thought, remembering that it was God who had allowed them to be separated in the first place.

She couldn't argue that it was impressive what he'd been through to return home. And he was right. He was returning home to see his family. But was that truly God's doing? She'd been the one to agree to let him go. She could have taken him straight to Langley and let them sort all this out. Shouldn't she be the one he was thanking instead of God?

And while Marcus was making his journey across the globe, she'd spent the past few years living in limbo while she'd searched for her own answers. Her quest had always led her to only more questions. If God had been guiding Marcus, bringing him back home, then what had He been doing for Bethany?

Erecting roadblocks everywhere she went and wasting her time following up on leads that went nowhere, that's what.

She released an angry breath. She had spent the past year pedaling like a hamster on a wheel in vain with nothing to show for it. And why would a kind and loving God separate them two years ago only to bring them back together now under these untenable circumstances? As far as she was concerned, God was *not* fighting for her.

And now, despite Marcus right in front of her, Bethany felt more alone than she'd ever been. She went back to her room and fell asleep wishing she knew for certain one way or another if she could trust him.

He could see last night's conversation was still weighing heavily on her as they stopped the next morning for a quick breakfast before continuing. Yet as he sat across from her munching on a sausage and biscuit, she tried to pretend she hadn't been affected by his words about faith and God. She seemed so hostile toward faith and that bothered him in a way he couldn't fully comprehend. Why should it matter to him what her relationship with the Lord was like?

He knew the truth of his question. There was so much more to their relationship than she'd shared with him. He felt it every time he was with her. She'd already alluded to the fact that he'd hurt her when he'd left, but he suspected it had more to do with just his supposed dying in Afghanistan. Had his death somehow driven her away from God? Or had she never been there at all? And what did that say about his relationship with the Lord preambush?

"I want to show you something," she said, pulling up Facebook, scrolling through then handing her phone to him. "It's your sister Shannon's profile page. I thought you might want to look through it before we arrive there."

He scrolled through the photos of a woman with dirty blond hair, big green eyes and a broad, happy smile. In several photos she'd labeled "Me and Marcus" he saw his face staring back, a happy, content smile of someone who knew who he was and was satisfied with his life. He saw a resemblance between them and his heart clenched to see actual proof of his past life.

"She's pretty."

"Yes, she's a teacher at the high school. She lives with your mom in the same house where you both grew up. Apparently, you were very close."

"How do you know so much about my life?"

He hoped she might open up more about their relationship, but instead she only shrugged. "When I realized you might be alive, I dug through everything I could find about your background, including your mother and sister. I had to make sure you weren't funneling money to them."

Something about the callous way she spoke, as if it had all been just another part of her job, rubbed him wrong. "You had no right to do that."

Her eyes widened in surprise. "I had *every* right. At the time I believed you were a government spy passing secrets to the enemy. I couldn't prove it, but I believed it. I took every measure I could possibly get access to. There were some areas I couldn't access. I was denied entry to your emails. The problem was I couldn't prove you were alive and the US government had declared you KIA, remains unrecoverable based on the testimony of the other rangers, specifically Garrett Lewis."

He knew the name from looking through the files and remembering that Bethany had told him back at the police station that he and Garrett had been close friends. "Why? What did he say?"

"He claimed he saw your body after an explosion. He ran to help you but knew before he reached you that it was too late. You weren't moving. Unfortunately for you, he never made it to you. He came across one of the other survivors, Levi Thompson, who was seriously injured, and knew he had to get him to safety."

"Did Levi survive?"

"Yes. He was badly injured and was given a medical discharge. I understand he's undergone multiple surgeries related to his injuries, but I'd say Garrett saved his life that day." Her face softened and a bit of compassion shone through. "Garrett's account is the last known sighting of you, Marcus."

"What about Levi? Can he confirm Garrett's account of that night?"

"No. He suffered severe head trauma. He doesn't remember a thing about the night of the ambush."

It seemed pretty convenient to him that the only official report of his demise had come from one soldier. Had something happened between them and Garrett was covering his tracks by claiming Marcus had been killed? Or had he truly thought him dead? By all reports, they had been the best of friends, but Marcus knew even good friends fought and a lot could happen in the heat of an argument.

His mind began imagining all sorts of scenarios. A fight that ended in bloodshed. Perhaps Garrett believed he'd killed him and then the ambush had helped to cover his deed. He shook his head. That's all it was… conjecture. He had no proof and he certainly had no memory of such an event. It was possible, even probable, that's Garrett's account of the night of the ambush was exactly the way it had happened.

He ran his hands through his hair, frustration taking a big ole bite of his soul. He needed answers. Why couldn't he remember? He willed his mind to recall that night but nothing came. Only a big wall that he couldn't climb, blocking his access to his life.

She crumpled her paper wrapper then stood. "We're only an hour away from your mother's house. Are you ready for this?"

He nodded and stood, taking both their trays to the trash. He didn't know how ready he actually was to face a family he knew only through their photos and CIA-gathered information, but he was anxious to get there, to see the house he grew up in and, most important, to discover if doing so brought back any memories.

They were both quiet on the rest of the trip into Waco. Marcus checked behind them frequently to make certain they weren't being followed while Bethany used the GPS on her phone to give him directions to the address. His heart started pounding as they turned onto the street bearing the house where he'd grown up. Nothing on the tree-lined street with its modest middle-class homes seemed familiar to him. He'd hoped for some recognition of the place where he'd spent his formative years. But as he pulled up to the curb in front of the house bearing the address 1420 Marlen Street, he was still unaffected by the scenery.

"Your mother's name is Elizabeth Allen. Your father died when you were twelve and she raised you and your sister alone."

Marcus searched his mind for some image, some spark of memory, but all he got was a blank. "I have no recollection of either one of them," he told her. "And I'm about to change their lives." His family still thought he was dead, and Marcus was about to knock on their door with no warning. It wasn't fair springing this on them this way and guilt washed through him. "We should have called first."

Bethany reached out and touched his arm, her fingers enflaming his heart at their mere touch. He was surprised by the warmth of her comforting gesture. "They'll be so happy to see you alive, they won't even care."

As they got out, the front door opened and the woman he'd seen on her profile page—his sister, Shannon—stepped outside. She was juggling a travel coffee mug and a handful of papers in her hands and digging through her bag, so she didn't spot them immediately as she headed for the car in the driveway.

His heart felt as if it would burst at any moment when he saw her, but it was out of fear and anxiety more than recognition. He searched his mind for some memory of them together but there was nothing.

The woman seemed to notice the truck parked in front of her house. She stopped and glanced their way, spotting Bethany first as she slid out of the passenger's seat. Her face seemed to register recognition and her eyes widened in surprise. He saw her start to speak but then her eyes landed on Marcus as he moved around the front of the truck to the driveway and she stopped. Her face paled and a cry caught in her throat.

"I don't believe it," she said softly, but Marcus heard her words.

He took several more cautious steps toward her and watched her struggle with both joy and apprehension. Tears filled her eyes and her hands shook. "Marcus!" she cried, dropping her armful of items and sprinting across the lawn to where he stood. She threw her arms around him. "You're alive," she cried. "I can't believe it. You're really alive."

He embraced her, pulling her tighter against him. He still didn't know her, but was swept up into the emotion of the moment. "It's me, Shannon," he told her hoarsely. "It's really me."

She broke from his hold, turned and ran back across the lawn, shouting at the top of her lungs, "Mama! Come quickly. It's Marcus!"

His gut clenched as another woman appeared in the doorway. She was older than Shannon and her face held worry lines. Had he caused those? Her expression now was full of concern and he imaged Shannon had frightened her half to death with her screaming.

"What's going on?" she asked as she slipped outside. "What's the matter?"

Shannon grabbed her arm and spun her to face him.

Marcus suddenly felt exposed. How would she react to his returning from the dead this way? Shock registered on her face and she started toward them. He closed the distance and met her at the concrete steps leading up to the house. She still looked confused as she stared at him and, for a brief moment, it frightened him. Did he have the wrong house? Had Bethany gathered incorrect information about him? Was their dead son and brother actually another man?

Elizabeth Allen lifted her hand and touched his cheek. He smiled at the gentle feel of her fingers on his skin. It did seem familiar but it was more of an instinctual feeling instead of an actual memory, as if she'd done it so many times in his life that his skin instinctively knew the feel of her touch. He placed his hand over hers and she smiled.

"My boy," she whispered brokenly. "You're home. You're finally home."

Her simple words struck a chord in him, as if soothing an open wound inside his soul. Although he still did not know them, he was finally getting answers he'd spent so long searching for. He pulled her into a hug and thanked God for finally leading him home.

Bethany folded her arms, uncomfortable at the open display of emotion while standing outside on the lawn.

She was glad when Shannon opened the front door and motioned them all inside. She did not know if Marcus was being gracious or if he actually remembered them, but it was obvious from their reactions that they had not seen or heard from him in years. They'd believed he was dead. She followed them inside and closed the door. The house was furnished with simple colors and comfortable furnishings. Nothing fancy, and she got the feeling from being there that this was a family that didn't feel the need to put on pretense. She liked that. On the walls and bookshelves were family photos and pictures of Marcus at all stages of his life. Front and center on the mantel was one of him in his official army ranger regalia.

"I don't understand," his mother said, pulling him to a seat beside her on the couch as tears of joy slid from her eyes. She wiped them away. "What happened to you? Where have you been, Marcus? The army told us you'd died in combat."

Shannon shook her head in disgust. "I can't believe we trusted them."

"It's not the army's fault. Everyone thought I had died." He glanced Bethany's way then gave a wry smile. "Well, almost everyone." He stood and moved to where she stood by the fireplace. "This is Bethany Bryant. She works for the CIA. She's the one who tracked me down."

Shannon gave him a confused look. "What do you mean she tracked you down? Where have you been, Marcus? Were you captured? Have you been in captivity all this time?"

"No, nothing like that. I was injured in the ambush, but I didn't die. A family of villagers found me. They kept me alive and helped me get back to the States. I had no idea who I was. I still don't know. I don't remember this house or any of these photos and, I'm very sorry, but I don't know either of you, either."

Elizabeth Allen gasped in shock but Shannon was the one who expressed it. "You don't remember us? Are you saying you have amnesia?"

He nodded. "I do."

She looked at Bethany. "Where did you find him?"

"He was working as a grill cook at a diner in Little Falls."

Shannon blanched and fell back onto the sofa cushions. "Are you telling me you've been only a few hours away from us all this time?"

His face reddened as if he had done something wrong. Bethany didn't miss it.

"For the last several months, yes."

Shannon shook her head, her brain obviously still trying to comprehend it all. Suddenly she stood. "I've got to go call the school and let them know I won't be in today."

Bethany stopped her before she walked out of the room. "Would you mind not telling them why, for the time being? We don't need the publicity a back-from-the-dead-brother feature story might bring."

Shannon stared at her then a knowing look seeped into her expression. She glanced at Marcus then back at Bethany. "Why? Is he in some kind of trouble?"

"I just think it would be best for now."

She gave a resigned nod then left the room. Bethany knew they would have to have a conversation about the gravity of what Marcus was facing but not now, not in front of his mother. How could she tell this family that he might be a traitor? Or that, at the very least, someone was trying to kill him to stop him from telling what he didn't even know?

She glanced at Marcus, who gave her a nod of appreciation, then turned his attention to his mother, who pounded him with questions.

She'd seen emotion on his face, but he'd been calm and collected. Seeing that helped her feel better about her decision to trust him. Either he really did have amnesia or he was a psychopath with no feelings. Anyone who would put their family through what these ladies had been through on purpose would have to be incredibly coldhearted.

Bethany watched him with his mother and a pang of jealousy hit her. Being here in his home and seeing his family's reaction to discovering he was alive—this family had had the reunion she'd always hoped for. There had been a time she would have been the one flinging herself into Marcus's arms and being so happy to see him again. But all she'd felt when she'd seen him alive was anger and betrayal.

She heard Shannon on the phone and went to find her in the kitchen. When she hung up, her eyes remained on Bethany. Finally she beckoned her to join her. Curious, Bethany did.

"I know who you are," Shannon told her. It sounded

more like an accusation than a statement, as if she were saying, "I know what you did."

"I told you who I am."

"Yes, I know. You work for the CIA. You tracked down Marcus and are helping him recover his memories." She shook her head and leaned in close to Bethany. "But I know who you *really* are."

Shannon walked to the cabinet, opened a drawer and returned with a small item in her hand. Bethany saw it was a phone. Shannon powered it on, clicked on a button and turned it toward Bethany.

Her heart stopped at what she saw. The background screen was a photo of Marcus and a woman kissing and posing for a selfie.

"That's you," Shannon stated.

Bethany couldn't deny it.

She gasped, remembering the day that photo had been taken, reliving every precious moment. The feel of his arms around her. The smell of his aftershave. And, most important, his adoring words as he'd snapped that picture. *I want to remember this moment forever.*

She'd protested. After all, she couldn't have her photo taken while she was working covertly. He'd promised to delete it, but it had been a mistake to let him take it in the first place. In fact, their entire relationship had been a no-no. They both could have found themselves in big trouble.

She took the phone from Shannon and looked closer at the photo. Tears pressed against her eyes. That had been a sweet memory for her, but one that had been dashed by Marcus's betrayal.

"That's Marcus's phone. We received it from the army with his personal belongings. You knew my brother before the attack, didn't you?"

Bethany gulped away the tears and tried to remain composed. "Yes, I did."

"I've stared at that picture over and over again and wondered about that woman. Who was she? He never told me he'd met someone. I always thought if I could find this woman, I might have some insight into what Marcus's last few days were like."

Bethany pressed a button on the phone to shut off the image. She wasn't there to damage the image Shannon had of her brother. In her eyes, he was a hero. Bethany hated the idea that Shannon might have to face the same truth she was now living: learning that Marcus might not be the patriot they'd all believed him to be.

But that reality didn't have to hit today. "It was a relatively new relationship," she told Shannon. "I met your brother only two weeks before the ambush. We barely had time to get to know one another."

She glanced at the photo again. "Looks like you knew him well enough."

"Marcus doesn't know about our past relationship," Bethany said. "He doesn't remember and I haven't told him."

"Why not?"

She closed her eyes and remembered the feel of being wrapped in his arms and the whisper touch of his lips on hers. She pushed away those memories. That was a long time ago. It was time to leave it in the past. "I've moved on, Shannon. I made a new life, one that doesn't include Marcus." It wasn't true, but she couldn't give false hope to anyone that she and Marcus could ever have a future together.

She realized the truth. She couldn't even give it to herself.

The bright Texas sun shone down on him. Marcus lifted his head and soaked it in as he stood in the backyard. It had been his mother's suggestion that they sit outside by the pool and it hadn't even occurred to him that it might be too cool to do so. This was Texas, after all, and the temps fluctuated from day to day. He was thankful the weather was warm enough for this and imagined spending summers in the pool and enjoying family barbecues. Of course, he had to imagine it all because he still didn't remember.

Marcus glanced at the grill and knew he could operate it as if he'd done it a million times. He supposed it was like falling off a bike. Having amnesia did not preclude him knowing how to operate a gas grill any more than recalling the ins and out of working a .300 Win Mag sniper rifle.

He turned as the back door opened and the three women walked out. Shannon was carrying a tray with glasses and a pitcher of what he assumed to be sweet tea. He could almost taste it and felt a memory of drinking his mama's sweet tea trying to surface.

Bethany carried a photo album and was smiling and laughing as Elizabeth pointed out photos—no doubt of him—as they stepped outside. He enjoyed the way her blue eyes lit up when she laughed.

Man, she was beautiful.

He didn't yet know Elizabeth or Shannon well, but he was certain the women standing before him were the most important women in his life both pre and post ambush.

Elizabeth's face clouded as she turned the page. "This was my husband, David. Marcus and Shannon's father," she said, pointing to a photo. "He was a mechanic in the army for eight years. He would have been so proud of his son becoming an army ranger." She glanced up at him and smiled. "We were all so very proud."

Had he joined up because of his dad? He had so many questions. Would he ever know the answers to any of them?

As Shannon set the tray on a patio table, Bethany pulled the photo out and walked to Marcus, showing it to him. He saw a man about his age in green army fatigues.

"You look like him," Bethany said softly, and he nodded.

"I see the resemblance." They shared the same light-colored hair and strong chin. Marcus saw similar features in Shannon, as well. He imagined there were many more resemblances that weren't physical.

"I like your family," Bethany murmured. "They seem to care a great deal about you."

He stared into her eyes and was filled with a rush of gratitude. She'd found him, given him back his name and allowed him to search for his family. "I wouldn't even know them if it wasn't for you," he said and meant it. "Thank you for this."

"Anything coming back to you yet?"

"No, not yet, but I feel like I'm on the verge of something. Like it's right there and I only have to reach out and grab the truth." He glanced at her. He'd felt that way with Bethany since the first moment he'd laid eyes on her. She was so wrapped up in his past that he could not imagine she wasn't a vital part of it. He touched her hand and let his fingers entwine with hers. She didn't pull away, which gave him hope that someday she could learn to trust him again. She was important to him. If he discovered nothing else about his life, he was certain of that.

"I don't want to be a part of this anymore," she told him. He had a moment of panic that she was regretting bringing him here and being here with him. "I thought I was doing the right thing by finding you and taking you back to the Agency, but now I can't do it. I just can't do it, Marcus."

"You can do it, Bethany, and you will. You have a duty to your job and to your country. My only regret is that I've put you in this situation. I'm sorry for the pain I've caused you. I have to trust that, if I did these things, God is allowing me to face the consequences of my actions and, if I didn't, that He's leading me to the truth so I can be exonerated." He swallowed hard. "I don't know what kind of future He has in store for me, but I trust that He can and will fix it for me. I have no clue what that will look like, but I have faith that God will work it all out."

He nearly added that he hoped God would work it all out for them, as well, but he saw the hesitation already rising in her eyes as he spoke about God and faith. Probably not a good idea to get too far ahead of himself.

Marcus noticed the tea was gone from her glass. He took it from her and rattled the remaining ice. "Why don't I go refill this for you?"

A popping noise shook the air. Marcus dropped the glass and instinctively grabbed for his gun, every sense now on alert. His mother and sister gasped at his sudden action, but he didn't see the same kind of panic in Bethany's face as he scanned the area.

She placed a reassuring hand on his arm. "It's okay, Marcus."

"I'm sure it was only a car backfiring," Shannon said, worry clearly coming through in her tone.

He glanced at her. She was clinging to his mother, who looked frightened. They probably were wondering if he was suffering PTSD because they didn't know what he and Bethany had been through in the past two days.

"It's okay, Marcus," Bethany told him again, this time her tone more calming. "We're okay."

He lowered the gun then put it away, but his senses were on alert and a deep rumbling in the pit of his stomach told him something was wrong. It was a familiar feeling and one he was certain had rarely let him down. Every sound that drifted over the air, every dog bark and sound of a car driving by, raised the tension of the moment.

This is crazy, he thought. *I'm building up something*

that means nothing. When he spotted the familiar red targeting laser trained on Bethany's back, he knew with a sickening pang that he was right.

The shot fired, hitting her before he could do anything to stop it. The force of the bullet sent her reeling forward into the pool. The splash of the water as she hit it sounded like a tidal wave to his ears. He hurtled himself to the ground to pull her out but three more shots blocked his way and he scrambled back, taking cover behind a metal chair.

Bethany! He had to get to her.

Screams from his mother and sister, now huddled beneath the patio table, grabbed his attention. Fear was written across their faces. They hadn't asked for this, hadn't asked him to bring a killer to their home.

"Get inside and call 9-1-1," he told them, drawing his gun and returning the sniper's fire.

As instructed, the women crawled out from under the table and ran for the door. Marcus continued firing, crouching behind the chair and using it as a shield as he crawled to the edge of the pool. His heart dropped when all he saw was empty water tinged red.

"I'm here," Bethany said softly, causing him to turn. She was crouched in the corner of the pool, her head barely above water.

His heart soared at the sight of her. "Are you okay? There's blood in the water."

"It's just a shoulder wound. I'll be all right."

Pocketing his gun, he reached for her and pulled her out of the pool, water dripping and sloshing.

"Where is he?" she asked.

"On the roof two doors down. We have to get inside."

She nodded as he took out his gun and then ran when he started firing. He took off behind her, shooting aimlessly in the sniper's direction.

The shooter ignored Marcus's shots and fired, too, several bullets hitting too close to them as they dashed across the patio.

Bethany didn't stop or hesitate and Marcus was glad he didn't have to remind her to keep moving. She sprinted across the patio stones, slung open the back door and hurried inside, slamming it shut once Marcus crossed the threshold.

He hurried into the living room, bolted the front door then closed the curtains, being careful to stay to the side of the window. Bethany helped him, but he realized the house had too many windows to cover them all. A row of glass lined one wall in the dining room alone. Those would be difficult to cover since there were no curtains.

"We're too exposed," Bethany said and he agreed.

Two figures emerged from the kitchen and Marcus had his weapon in his hand ready to fire until his mother's cry stopped him.

"What's going on?" Shannon demanded. "What's happening?"

"Get downstairs in the basement," he ordered. "You're safer down there."

Bethany locked eyes with them. "Maybe we all are? A contained room with no windows?"

Marcus shook his head. "We'll be sitting ducks."

"We kind of already are."

He turned to his mother. "Did you call the police?"

She nodded. "They're on their way."

"Good. Now, get back downstairs. You're safer there." He ushered his mother and sister back through the basement door and instructed them to lock it from the inside. He grabbed a dish towel and pressed it into her shoulder wound, causing her to grimace in pain. "Hold that there as long as you can. Our only hope is to fight him off until the police arrive. I won't let him get to my family."

Bethany nodded. "Maybe he won't come in at all. He'll just wait for us to come out. Aren't snipers trained to keep their positions until their targets emerge?"

"They are, but I'm not so sure anymore that this guy is formally trained."

"Why do you say that?"

"He's taken a lot of shots and none of them have hit us."

She snorted and motioned at her arm. "Speak for yourself."

"What I mean is he hasn't killed us yet. He's sloppy and impulsive. Military-trained snipers are patient. They wait for the right target. Think about the chaos he caused back at the diner. Even the bomb from the airplane was homemade. We were operating under the assumption that he used whatever was on hand to create it, but what if that's all he has to use? He might not have the knowledge to create a more sophisticated weapon."

"Sophisticated or not, it did the job. It killed the pilot," she reminded him.

"I'm not saying he's not dangerous, Bethany, only that he might not be professionally trained." It was something to ponder.

"How does that help—" Her words were cut off when something burst through one of the dining room windows and a small metal container rolled across the floor.

"It's a smoke bomb," she yelled as a white fog began to hiss from the cylinder.

He covered his mouth and nose and hurried into the kitchen, pulling open drawer after drawer until he found more towels. "He's coming inside," he told her, turning on the water in the sink and dousing the towels. His eyes were already burning from the smoke that was steadily taking over the rooms. "Place this over your mouth and nose."

She coughed, an indication that the smoke was doing its job. "We have to get out of here," she said urgently. "If he was close enough to throw the smoke bomb, then he's not in sniper position. Now's our chance."

Before he could respond, the front door burst open and a man entered. He was wearing a gas mask. They both hit the floor as he opened fire and sprayed the rooms with bullets.

Marcus saw Bethany holding her ears from the noise of the gun. She then used the cover of the smoke to crawl into the dining room and crouch beneath the table. He realized then that he knew how to make the smoke work for him.

The sniper wore a gas mask, which protected his face but would not do anything to help his vision. Marcus circled the kitchen island, careful to remain low and out of sight as the attacker moved past it. When he turned and headed back the other way, Marcus swiped his legs, knocking the man to his knees.

He jumped up and tackled him, sending the rifle sliding several feet away. The sniper scrambled for it but Marcus grabbed him and pulled him back, trying to dodge the man's kicks to his face. One connected and Marcus released his grip at the pain of a man-size boot ramming into his jaw. His eyes watered briefly but he couldn't be sure if that was from the pain of the kick or the smoke that had filled the room.

The sniper grabbed his rifle and slammed the butt into Marcus's cheek. Pain ripped through him and he fell back as the man leaped to his feet and stood over Marcus.

"I've got you now," he said, raising the gun to Marcus's face. Marcus stared down the barrel and knew this was it. He was about to die.

SIX

Bethany jumped to her feet and sprinted across the kitchen, leaping into the air and landing hard on the sniper's back before he could fire. Startled, he dropped the weapon as she dug her nails into his neck. Yelping, the assailant reached behind him, grabbed her arm, pulling her forward and flipping her. She hit the floor with a thud before he reached for her, pulled her up and tossed her against the counter. Evil radiated from him as he wrapped his hands around her neck and started choking her.

She struggled to free herself but quickly realized she was no match for his strength. That didn't mean she was going down without a fight. She flung out her arms, reaching for anything on the countertop to use as a weapon. Her hand closed around something narrow and sharp—a meat thermometer—and she dug it deep into her attacker's arm. He cried out in pain and loosened his grip. She gasped for air, coughing and trying to catch her breath. He grabbed at his arm, stared at the cut she'd given him, then clutched her again, his fingers digging into her neck before she could escape.

Suddenly, Marcus appeared behind him, raised his hands and slammed an iron skillet across the back of the guy's head. The force sent the man to his knees then to the floor, squirming in pain.

Marcus leaned against the counter and gently framed her face in his hands. "Are you okay?" he rasped.

Her throat was on fire and her was neck tender. When she tried to speak to tell him she was fine, she couldn't. Instead she simply nodded to let him know she was okay. Sirens roared in the distance and she was thankful for the sound.

Their attacker heard them, too. He stumbled to his feet and raced to the back door, slinging it open and taking off running. Marcus swooped up the rifle and chased after him.

Suddenly the house seemed quiet after the hustle and bustle of the last few minutes. Bethany heard a voice calling for help and remembered Elizabeth and Shannon in the basement. She pulled open the door, surprised that it wasn't locked anymore because she was certain Marcus had made them secure it from the inside.

She saw the two women at the bottom of the stairs. Shannon was crying and looked up at her, panic written across her face. Elizabeth was slumped against her.

"You have to help us," Shannon cried. "She's been shot."

Bethany hurried down the steps and ran to them. She checked Elizabeth and saw blood pooling around her abdomen. "How did this happen?" she asked Shannon.

"I don't know. We were huddling down here like Marcus said to do when the shooting started. I guess one of the bullets came through the floor and hit her. She just collapsed right in front of me. I unlocked the door to get help but you and Marcus were fighting with that man and the house was full of smoke."

Bethany heard the sirens grow close then heard the sounds of cars stopping in front of the house. "The police are here. Don't worry. We'll get her to the hospital."

Bethany heard footsteps on the stairs behind her and turned. Marcus rushed to them. "Where is the shooter?" she asked.

"He got away. What happened?" he demanded, motioning to his mother on the floor.

"She's been shot. She needs an ambulance."

Marcus rushed back upstairs and returned a moment later with the paramedics, who had just arrived. She watched him as they tended to Elizabeth. His shoulders were tense and his jaw clenched, evidence that he was scared. It wasn't her mother suffering yet she still felt helpless as she watched the woman struggling for each breath. Relief only flowed through Bethany when they finally had her loaded into the ambulance.

Shannon crawled into the ambulance and rode with her to the hospital while Marcus and Bethany followed behind them after a brief discussion with the authorities. There would be more questions from the police and even from Shannon and Elizabeth, but for now the interrogation could wait. Bethany slid across the seat and put her head on his shoulder as he drove. "Everything is going to be fine," she soothed. He nodded, indicating he'd heard her, but she could see he didn't believe it.

She only wished she did.

Marcus pounded his fist against the steering wheel, angry and frustrated. He had no more of a clue as to who was doing this to him than they had before. He tried to be thankful they'd escaped in time…at least, he hoped they'd been in time. If that maniac had taken his mother from him before he'd even gotten to know her, Marcus would make sure he paid for it.

Bethany touched his arm, trying to be reassuring. "I'm sure she'll be fine," she said.

He wanted to believe she had some medical knowledge that he was unaware of, but she didn't. She was only trying to be encouraging. He couldn't stand the helplessness he'd felt standing there watching as his mother struggled for breath because someone was after him.

He pulled into the hospital parking lot and rushed inside. Bethany practically had to run to catch up. After asking the desk clerk for information about Elizabeth's condition, he scowled when he was told to take a seat and that someone would be out as soon as they knew something.

His realized his faith was wavering as he lowered himself into a chair. It wasn't fair and it wasn't right that his mother was suffering because of him. She hadn't asked for this and he hadn't meant to bring it into her life. He should have realized the danger after Milo and Marie had been killed, but he'd just been so caught up in learning about his past that he hadn't allowed the risks to his family to override his need for answers.

Bethany sat beside him and her presence was a great comfort to him, greater than she could possibly imagine. The waiting seemed never ending and more than once he stood and paced the waiting room before returning to his chair.

Finally, Shannon emerged from the back and updated them about Elizabeth's condition.

"She's going to be fine. Apparently, the bullet went straight through her. They want to keep her overnight, but they don't believe there is any lasting damage."

He blew out a quavering breath and silently lifted a prayer. *Thank You, God, for sparing her.*

"I'm going to remain with her tonight." His sister pulled out her keys, peeled off one and handed it to Marcus. "This is the key to the house. I don't even know that we locked it up, but in case someone did, this will get you inside."

A weight lifted from his heart at hearing his mother was going to be okay, but the relief quickly morphed into something cold and hard in the pit of his stomach.

"I know that look," Bethany whispered from beside him. "What are you thinking, Marcus?"

He wanted to ask her how she knew his look. That implied some kind of intimate knowledge of him. He thought again about that kiss and wondered for not the first time if she was being completely honest with him about their past relationship. But he couldn't even think about that right now. He had to put all that aside and focus on what was best for his family. And, as much as he wanted to stay and get to know these two women again, it was time for him to leave.

"We can't stay here," he told her. "I'm putting my family at risk the longer I stay."

Shannon didn't argue the point, which only made him more certain he was right. Their being here was a danger to his mother and sister. They had to leave.

He closed the hand Shannon held out. "We won't be needing this."

She grabbed his arm. "Yes, you will." She pulled him aside. "There's a box in the china cabinet in the kitchen. It has the personal items the army returned to us. Something in there may help you figure out why this is happening to you."

She placed the key into his hand. "Don't disappear on us again, Marcus, okay? Mom and I wouldn't be able to stand losing you again."

"You understand why I can't stay, don't you?"

She nodded. "I don't like it, but I do understand. You've always been the kind of man who puts other people before his own wants and desires. That, I'm proud to see, hasn't changed."

He pulled her into a hug, hating that he was once again leaving. But he knew where his family was now and he was determined he would make it back to his mom and sister one day soon. They had a lot of catching up to do.

He watched Shannon disappear through the double doors that led to the treatment area then turned and headed out. Bethany fell into step beside him. She'd graciously hung back when Shannon had pulled him aside, but now she was right by his side again.

"Where are we going?" she asked him.

"To the house to pick up something first. Shannon said it was my personal belongings. Maybe something in there will help shed some light on this situation. So far, I haven't found anything here that can tell me what happened the night of the ambush." He glanced her way. "If whatever's in that box doesn't answer some questions, then I need to speak with someone that was there that night. I know your files were destroyed back at Milo's, but do you remember anything about the other surviving rangers?"

"I've studied those files over and over for the past eighteen months. Trust me. I know everything that's inside them."

"Then I think it's time for me to meet my former comrades."

Bethany felt her face flush when Marcus left the house carrying a box containing his belongings. She knew what was inside…the cell phone with her photo. Shannon had showed it to her. How long until Marcus saw it, as well?

She shook her head. She couldn't worry about that now. If it came up, she would simply tell him that that was the past and they had no relationship anymore.

Her gut clenched even thinking about it. It wasn't true. Despite her best efforts, she couldn't deny she'd begun to trust Marcus again. She shuddered, remembering the feel of his hand on her skin when he'd examined her ankle. She recalled longing for more once he'd moved his hand away. Stop it, she told herself. She couldn't fall for those green eyes or his gentle touch again.

But she *was* falling. She couldn't deny it. From the moment she'd seen him again, all those old feelings had come rushing back to her. She wanted to believe in him, wanted to trust that he hadn't been involved with treasonous activities. She wanted him to be a good man.

God, please let him be good.

It was the first time she'd asked the Almighty for anything in a long, long time, but she didn't try to take it back. She wanted it too badly.

"Do you want me to drive?" he asked.

Bethany handed over the keys and then realized how easily even that decision had come to her.

She slid into the passenger's seat while he got behind the wheel. "So where are we going?" he asked.

She knew each of the surviving ranger's names, backgrounds and locations by heart, but that didn't mean she'd also memorized their exact addresses. She had already tried looking them up online to no avail, so she pulled out her phone to call Rick for the address. "Colton Blackwell lives in Louisiana. We should start there. I'll phone Rick and see if he can hunt down an exact address for us." She started dialing then realized Marcus was staring at her with a concerned look on his face. "What's the matter?"

He zeroed in on the cell in her hand. "Your phone. He's been tracking it. That must be how he keeps finding us."

"Impossible. This is a CIA-issued secure line. It's untraceable except by the highest levels of CIA security."

He locked eyes with her and suddenly she realized what he was thinking. Whoever was after them had classified CIA clearance or had someone in the Agency passing him information.

"I'll call Rick." She finished dialing then outlined the situation when her supervisor answered. "This guy seems to find us no matter where we go."

"Now, Bethany," Rick intoned. "I think you're jumping to conclusions. Surely, tracking down Marcus's family wasn't much of a stretch. He must have known you'd go there—" his voice became gravelly "—despite my direct orders that you bring him back to Langley."

She grimaced at his scolding. "I know, I know, but he wanted to come, hoping to learn more about his past."

"Has he remembered anything?"

"Not yet. Our next step is to contact the surviving rangers from his team and speak with them. That's really why I'm calling. I was hoping you could find a current address for Colton Blackwell. He was one of the members of Marcus's team."

"They've all been fully vetted about that night. Everything they know, we know."

"Possibly, but we both know that soldiers talk to one another more freely than they talk to officials or write reports. It's worth a shot."

"Bethany, I can't stress this enough. We need to know whatever Marcus knows about the night of the ambush. You have to help him regain his memories."

"So does that mean you now believe he has amnesia?" She glanced at Marcus, who was hanging on her every word.

"I trust you, Bethany. If you believe it, then I'm trusting in your judgment."

Releasing a pent-up breath, she locked eyes with Marcus and gave him an unsteady smile. She believed it. There was no doubt left in her mind that his memories of his life were gone, buried. She still could not say what he'd been doing the night of the ambush, but she believed he didn't know, either, and that at least was a comfort to her. "Can you access the files to see if anyone has been tracking my cell phone?"

She heard fingers clicking the keys of his computer. "Hmm, that's weird."

"What is it?"

"It looks like someone did access your phone files."

She gasped, surprised, and turned to Marcus. "Who was it, Rick?"

"Bill Donahue. A mid-level analyst from the terrorism task force."

Bethany didn't recognize the name. "What's his connection to Marcus or to me?"

She heard Rick's keyboard clicks again. "I don't see anything. It's so obscure that it strikes me as odd. I'm going to track down Agent Donahue and find out what he's been doing in those files and why. I'll get back to you afterward. I'll also see about getting you that address."

"Should I ditch the phone?"

"No, that's not necessary." She heard him typing again. "I'm adding another layer of security on your line. Now no one will be able to access your phone records without my approval."

"Thanks, Rick." Bethany pressed the off button and ended the call. Although she felt better knowing they could not be tracked with her phone, the name Rick had mentioned continued to haunt her. She didn't know anyone by that name. Why, then, was someone from the terrorism task force accessing her records and possibly following her around?

She turned and told Marcus about the find. "Any chance that name rings a bell?"

He furrowed his brow, thinking hard, then slowly shook his head. "It doesn't, but it doesn't mean Bill Donahue's not a part of this." He pressed a finger to the bridge of his nose and sighed. "Why can't I remember?"

His frustration was so palpable that it pierced her heart. She reached out for his hand and held it. "You will," she told him. "One day soon, you'll remember it all."

The smile on his lips spread all the way to his eyes and he squeezed her hand. "Do you really believe that, Bethany?"

"I do. And I'll be right there with you every step of the way."

Her phone buzzed with a text message from Rick. "It's an address for Colton Blackwell." She loaded the information into her maps app. "Looks like it's a six-and-half-hour drive. It'll be dark before we arrive there."

"Then I guess we'd better get going."

He put the truck into gear and they headed away from Waco and toward Louisiana.

They were an hour into the trip when her phone rang. She glanced at the screen and groaned.

"Who is it?" Marcus asked.

"My sister, Lisa." She'd made the mistake of agreeing to spend Christmas with Lisa and her husband last month. It had been a tediously pedestrian affair and Bethany had spent most of her time online working on her investigation, unaware how close she actually was to finding Marcus. She contemplated not answering it and even sent it to voice mail.

"You don't want to talk to her?"

"It's complicated." Her relationship with Lisa was a mess and she wasn't about to get into it with Marcus. She'd once shared such intimate family details with him but was hesitant to do so again.

"I can't ever thank you enough for reintroducing me to my sister. I may not remember her, but there's something different just knowing she's out there. I have someone I can count on now. It's a very satisfying feeling."

"Yes, well, your sister was happy to see you. From what I understand, you two always had a good relationship."

"Oh. I take it you and your sister don't get along?"

She hesitated. "It's not that we don't get along." She strained for the words to explain their relationship without really going into detail. "She doesn't approve of what I do."

"Really? She doesn't like that you work for the CIA?"

"I don't think its proper enough for her."

He gave her a confused glance. "What do you mean?"

"My sister has the perfect life. She married a lawyer, has two kids, the big house, the country club, all that."

"Sounds like you're jealous."

"No, I'm really not. I never wanted any of that despite my parents' constant pushing me to settle down, marry the right guy. Their vision of the perfect life isn't the same as mine."

He nodded as if he understood just how she felt. "So, what is *your* vision of the perfect life?"

"I love to travel and learn about other cultures. That's just not good enough for any of them."

"Maybe they just don't understand you."

"I'm sure they don't. They don't want to understand me, either." She didn't mention how much it hurt to know she was an outcast in her own family.

He patted the steering wheel. "You know, my sister said something to me. She told me she was always worried about me when I deployed. It was as if she was in a constant state of worry. She didn't like my job but how could she argue about protecting the country? Maybe your family feels that way, too. It sounds like your life frightens them and they don't know how to process it."

"I suppose that's right," she acknowledged. "They never made much of an effort, though."

"So, do they know about your covert work?"

"Oh, no. They think I travel to the Middle East to translate and negotiate logistics for military bases in the region. That in itself is dangerous enough for them." She rolled her eyes. "If they knew about my covert missions, they would really be beside themselves."

"So they believe you take risks because you enjoy it

instead of because you're trying to save lives. If they knew that, it might make a difference."

"I doubt it." Her phone rang again. It was her sister calling back. "Argh." She sent Lisa's call to voice mail again. "My family doesn't understand that accepting this desk job permanently is a demotion for me. I want to go back to field work one day, but I guess I'm just scared of it right now, you know?" She sighed. "Which suits them just fine because they don't seem to care how much I miss being in the field, traveling, meeting people, putting to use the skills I've spent years perfecting."

"It does sound like you miss it. How come you accepted a desk job then?"

She felt a hitch in her throat. How could she tell him she was physically unable to function in the field after losing him? She couldn't. She wouldn't. But there was another reason that had kept her out. "There was an investigation after the ambush and it was determined the translator that I vetted was really working for the enemy. He led our guys right in the ambush."

Her heart constricted as the unbidden memories flooded through her. "After that, I spent a lot of time trying to figure out what clues I'd missed about him. I thought he was a decent guy and my judgment got a lot of good men killed."

"It sounds like he fooled a lot of people, not just you."

"It was a few months later, after all the hubbub had calmed down, that I saw a report that this translator was found among the dead. The oversight committee concluded that he got caught up in the ambush and was accidentally killed.

"Only, Marcus, that's not what happened. I saw the photos and he was clearly executed. That really made me start wondering about him. Wondering, was I really wrong? Or was he being used as a scapegoat? I guess you could say that was the start of my investigation."

"So a dead translator led you to suspect corrupt soldiers, which led you to me."

She nodded. "I guess you could say that was the train of investigation."

He gave an amused smile that irked her. "What's that smirk about? Do I amuse you?"

"No, Bethany. You *amaze* me. When you were talking about your family, you were so tense and agitated. But when you started talking about the translator, the investigation, you lit up."

Her heart fluttered when she heard the unmistakable note of admiration in his tone.

"You seem very passionate about your work."

"I guess I am." Or rather, she used to be.

"So, I take it you're estranged from your family?" he asked. "That's a lonely life."

"I'm CIA. A solitary life is almost a given for the work I do."

"I doubt that's true. I bet many of your colleagues are married with families."

She couldn't deny that. Rick had been married for six years and had recently discovered his wife was pregnant. But he worked in the office full-time and rarely traveled. She couldn't think of one person in the covert analysis division who had been able to maintain a relationship. In fact, she knew of three whose spouses had filed for divorce in the past year. Perhaps that was why she and Dillon had been drawn together. They understood the job and the risks.

She checked her phone and noticed she had three missed calls from him as well as a text message that read Just checking in. Call me soon.

Bethany really needed to call him.

She glanced over at Marcus, remembering that she'd never had to find time to phone him. He had been on her mind constantly. She doubted it would have taken him three missed calls and a text message to get a response.

She had to stop.

Comparing them was futile. Dillon was stable and kind while Marcus made promises then left her high and dry.

Strangely enough, Dillon was just the kind of man her mother and father would approve of her dating. He exuded self-confidence and his cover job was as an attorney for an overseas oil company.

She could not even say for sure if that made Dillon the more attractive option or not.

SEVEN

Marcus let his mind wander as the music mingled with the sounds of the highway. The song on the radio held a steady beat and he thumped his finger to it against the steering wheel. It was a familiar tune. Although he didn't know, he felt certain he had a specific memory—a good memory—associated with the song. He glanced over at Bethany sleeping in the passenger's seat and wondered if she was a part of that memory.

There was something between them. He knew it. He felt it deep inside him. Even since the first time he'd seen her in the diner, he'd felt a stirring in his gut that this woman was something special to him. Just as certain as he knew he liked this song and this band, he knew Bethany Bryant was more to him than she seemed.

You might not like the answer, a voice deep inside warned him.

He didn't care. He only wanted to know the truth, to understand why his heart kicked up a notch when she touched him and why he seemed so powerfully drawn to her. He was a moth and she was the flame and, just like that moth, he couldn't stay away. A car roared up behind him, fast approaching and bearing down on him with its bright lights on. Marcus flipped the mirror so the light wouldn't be so blinding and slowed down, hoping the car would go around him. Tonight, he was willing to give the approaching vehicle a wide berth to pass.

But the car didn't go around him. Instead it roared up behind him and tapped him bumper to bumper.

Bethany awakened, startled by the sudden impact. "What's happening?" She glanced at the vehicle behind them. "Is that him?"

"I thought it was just a motorist. Now, I'm not so sure."

The car rammed them again and pushed the back wheels onto the shoulder. Marcus gripped the steering wheel, trying to level off, but the truck spun. He jerked the wheel and they were back on the street. Adrenaline pumping through him, he pushed the accelerator to the max and lengthened the distance between them.

Bethany took out her gun and checked it.

He reached to stop her hand as an image of some crazy, drag racing kid floated through his mind. "What if it's not him?"

She seemed to understand his concern and nodded. "I'll just fire a couple of warning shots."

She pulled down the window, leaned out and fired two shots. The truck swerved then came back faster and rammed them again.

She slid back inside. "It's our guy."

"Hang on."

He started maneuvering but the truck matched him move for move. They had to get away from this guy. He was too close to meeting up with Colton Blackwell and possibly learning something about his past.

Bethany was beside him, hanging on, gun still in her hand. He knew she was waiting for a smooth moment to lean out and start firing again, but he was focused on leaving this guy behind them and he knew he had the skills to lose him.

Suddenly shots rang out. The rear glass shattered and he lost control of the truck. It skidded and before Marcus could right it, the pickup slammed into them again, sending them flying from the road. The truck rolled, snapping his belt and tossing Marcus from his seat. Bethany's seat belt caught and she hung suspended in the air as the truck skittered down a slope and landed at the bottom.

Pain flickered through him as he landed against the overturned ceiling. A sticky residue he took to be blood flowed down his face. He'd probably reopened the cut on his forehead. At least, he hoped that was all it was.

Bethany unbuckled her belt and dropped to the floor. She knelt beside him. "You're bleeding."

"It's just a cut. I'll be fine. We have to get out of here. He'll be coming for us."

She nodded. He crawled out through the window and held out his hand to help her. From above, he heard the truck screech to a halt and a door open. He glanced up and saw a figure standing on the edge. Looking down at them, he'd obviously spotted them moving because he raised the rifle in his hand.

"Go!" Marcus shouted and took off running, pushing Bethany in front of him. They ducked into the trees as shots rang out. She didn't slow down and he booked it to keep up with her. He heard the rifle fire again and the shots were close enough that Marcus knew it would not be long before one of them was hit.

Bethany darted through the woods surrounding the road where they'd gone off. Roots jutting out from the ground made the terrain treacherous. Her ankle was still sore and she was tired of the running. When would it end? When would they finally be able to evade this sniper?

She ran by a creek and tripped. Marcus caught her, his strong arms wrapping around her before she hit the ground. Struggling to catch her breath, she stared up into his eyes and he pulled her close to him. She felt the rapid beating of his heart and her own heart jarred from something other than being tired and afraid. It had been so long since she'd been this close to him and it brought back memories—good memories—of the days before the ambush.

"You can let me go now," she told him, but even to her own ears, her voice sounded breathless. His arms tightened instead of releasing her and she felt her heart thundering in her chest. Why did he still have the ability to make her knees go weak? It wasn't fair. She didn't want to be attracted to him but her heart seemed to have a will of its own no matter how she tried to tame it.

"I feel like we've done this before," he said, his brow furrowed in confusion.

She moved her hands to his arms and pushed away from him, determined not to let her vulnerability show. "We can't stay in the woods," she told him. "We need to get back onto the road and hopefully flag someone down."

He nodded and took a step back, giving her the space she'd requested. The funny thing was, she missed his arms when they were no longer around her.

"He'll have the advantage without the trees for cover," Marcus said.

"I'd say he already has a distinct advantage."

They couldn't stay in these woods indefinitely. They needed to get to help and that meant getting up to the road and flagging down a car.

"What was the traffic like?" she asked, hating the fact that she'd slept through most of the drive.

"It wasn't busy, but it's still our best option. We're sitting ducks in these woods."

She nodded her agreement. "Let's go."

The embankment was steep so Marcus stayed behind as Bethany made the climb first. It was difficult and both her shoulder and ankle cried out in protest. Pushing through the pain, she grabbed for branches and rocks and heaved herself up.

She nearly slid back down the hill when shots rang out and pinged on a tree a few feet away. Screaming, she lost her footing. Marcus grabbed her and pushed her upward, following quickly behind. She saw the road ahead of her and willed herself to continue. She would not die in these woods. Not like this when they were so close to discovering the truth about Marcus and his past.

She grabbed hold of a rock and pushed herself forward, stumbling out into the road. Headlights spilled over her and the screech of tires cried out as the car that appeared out of nowhere tried to stop.

It hit her with a thump and pain ripped through her as she was thrown across the hood before sliding onto the pavement. The last thing she remembered before she lost consciousness was seeing Marcus running frantically toward her.

Marcus heard the screech of tires and the blare of a horn then the distinctive thump of something bad. Very bad. He scrambled to the top of the embankment and heaved himself over it.

Bethany lay sprawled on the pavement, glass surrounding her. A few feet away, skewered on the road, sat an SUV. The doors opened and a person slowly emerged from each side. Marcus ran to her, his heart pounding in fear. She wasn't moving. He dropped to his knees and felt for a pulse. He found one, steady and strong, and a rush of relief filled him. She wasn't dead.

Footsteps rushed up behind him and he acted instinctively, grabbing the gun he'd seen Bethany slip into her jacket. He jumped up and spun around, pointing it at the couple who looked stunned at the sight of a weapon.

The man spoke first. "Hey, bud, we just want to help. She ran out in front of my car."

"My name is Laura," the woman said soothingly. "I'm a nurse. She needs medical attention. Let me help her."

He summed them up quickly and determined they

weren't a threat. The woman was dressed in hospital scrubs and had probably just come from work or was heading there now. He lowered the gun and nodded, and she rushed past him to Bethany.

"Call 9-1-1," she said and the man pulled out his phone and dialed. His head popped up at a sound in the woods. "Are you two alone?"

"No," Marcus said. "Someone is out there. He ran us off the road and he was shooting at us."

The man went back to his SUV and pulled out a rifle then headed toward the woods. Marcus debated going with him but Bethany's gun did not have much ammo and he truly didn't want to leave her.

"How is she?" he asked, hovering over the woman's shoulder.

"I don't feel any broken bones but she may have hit her head or have internal injuries." She glanced up at Marcus. "Who's after you?"

He watched the trees for signs of the shooter. They weren't safe now, sitting unmoving on the road. They were an easy target.

The man returned from the woods. "Whoever was there is gone. I don't see any sign of him."

But Marcus didn't believe it. He felt the sniper's eyes on them. "He's still there, watching us, biding his time."

Bethany groaned and started stirring.

"She's coming to," the woman exclaimed and tried to hold Bethany's neck. "Calm down, sweetie. You've been in an accident. I'm an RN. I'm here to help you."

She didn't calm down. Instead she shouted, "Marcus!"

He fell to the ground beside her, taking her hand. "I'm here. I'm right here."

She held her head but tried to sit up. He saw her scan the trees. "We have to get out of here. He's still out there."

"I know. Can you stand?"

"I'll have to."

"I don't think that's a good idea," the nurse said. "You might have internal injuries."

"I'll have worse than that if we don't get out of here."

Marcus helped her to her feet then steadied her as her knees threated to buckle. He held her up.

"Take her to my car," the man stated.

Marcus walked with her, limping along, with him supporting her.

He helped her into the back seat and the woman climbed in beside her on the other side. "I want to keep an eye on her vitals until we reach the hospital. Drive slowly, Colton, you don't want to jar her."

Marcus's head spun around at the name she'd called him. "Colton? Are you Colton Blackwell?"

The man stopped and gave Marcus a hard stare. "Yeah, that's me. Why? Who are you?"

How was it possible that the very man they had come to see had found them instead? It could only be God's handiwork. "We were on our way to see you. My name is Marcus Allen. Do you know me?"

There was no denying the skeptical expression on the man's face as he moved his flashlight to get a better look at Marcus. He lowered the light but the wariness remained. "I used to know someone named Marcus Allen but he died."

"I know that's what everyone believed, but it's not true. I didn't die the night of the ambush."

Colton sighed then glanced into the back of the SUV. "Get in. I think we'd better get her to the hospital. We can work this all out later."

Marcus walked around and slid into the front passenger's seat. His heart was thundering in his chest as adrenaline and fear coursed through him. He turned to look at Bethany. Her face was full of pain and she was holding her right shoulder. He knew it was the one the sniper had grazed. His mind spun at all that was happening right now.

He reached for her hand and she responded similarly. He didn't want to let her go, but Bethany gave him a reassuring nod. "I'll be fine."

He wished he could believe her but he knew the truth. They wouldn't be fine until they uncovered who was trying to kill them—and why—and took him down.

This time it was Colton who paced back and forth in the ER waiting room while Marcus sat waiting for news.

The shock of the last hour was beginning to wear off and Marcus was tired, so tired. His heart had nearly stopped for good when he'd seen Bethany lying on the ground after being hit by the SUV.

Laura had ruled out any broken bones and Bethany had been talking and walking once she'd regained consciousness, so he wasn't that worried about her injuries, except for her shoulder. She'd given it quite an ordeal over the past few days.

Colton still hadn't asked him any questions, which seemed odd. Wouldn't he want to know how and why his former teammate was back from the dead? Everyone else seemed to want answers. Why didn't he?

The outside doors opened and Colton turned to greet a man in a police uniform. They shook hands and spoke quietly for a moment before Colton turned to Marcus, saying, "This is Sheriff Gil Martin. Gil, this is Marcus Allen. His girlfriend was the one I hit with the car."

Sheriff Martin shook Marcus's hand. "I have some questions I'd like to ask you both. But, first, has there been any word on the lady's condition?"

Marcus started to shake his head but the doors swung open and Laura appeared. He turned his focus to her instead. "How is she?"

"She's okay. She has some bumps and bruises but, honestly, she's in good shape. They want to keep her overnight for observation but—"

"Let me guess," Marcus said. "She's being stubborn." He chuckled and realized that was just like her.

Laura gave him a knowing smile. "Why, yes, she is. I told Dr. Shelby that I would keep an eye on her since I assume they'll be staying at the farmhouse." She glanced at Colton for verification and he nodded.

Marcus stopped her before she left again. "We didn't come here to intrude. Plus, you might have noticed by the way we met that someone is after us. It might not be safe for us to bring our problems to your home."

"It's safer if you stay with us," Colton said, giving

Laura the okay with a nod. She walked away and Colton turned his gaze back to Marcus. "It won't be the first time trouble has come looking for someone there. Believe me, we know how to handle it."

Sheriff Martin spoke. "I'm glad to see your lady friend is going to be okay. Will either of you be filing charges against Mr. Blackwell for running down your friend?"

"Hey," Colton said, shocked by the pronouncement. "I didn't exactly run her down. She ran from the woods and out in front of us. I couldn't stop."

"We won't be pressing charges," Marcus assured them both. "It was an accident."

Sheriff Martin nodded. "I'll call you both later to take your statements then for the paperwork."

"Will do. And say hello to your wife for me," Colton said.

The sheriff nodded and waved as he walked away. But he did not head outside. Instead he headed toward the back, presumably to question Bethany about the incident.

Colton turned and gave Marcus a curious glance. "I guess it's time you told me what's going on."

He rubbed a hand over his face. This was why he'd come here and why he'd tracked down Colton. He only wished seeing his former teammate had sparked some kind of memory. "My name is Marcus Allen."

"I know who you are, Marcus. I fought beside you for three years with the rangers. What I don't know is how you can possibly be here."

"I came searching for you, Colton. I need your help."

Colton locked him with a bewildered stare. "I thought you'd died, man. We all thought you were dead."

"I know. I was injured and some of the local villagers helped me. They tended to my wounds and hid me from the CIA. Someone in the Agency is recruiting soldiers to pass secrets to the enemy. Now they're after me."

"Why do they want you?"

"I don't know. I—I can't remember." He kneaded the back of his neck and sighed. "I think I might know something about their operation, only I can't remember what it is. Bethany is CIA. She's the one who found me. She's also led whoever is after us to me. They were shadowing her investigation and followed her to me. We've been dodging bullets ever since."

"What do you mean she *found* you?" Colton's brow furrowed in confusion. "Where were you, Marcus?"

He felt his face redden. "I can't remember what happened that night. In fact, I can't remember anything at all about my life. I have amnesia."

Colton gave him a sideways glance as if he didn't actually believe his tale. "What is it you think I can do to help you?"

"I don't know. I was hoping just seeing you, seeing someone from the team, would jog my memory, but it hasn't. It would help if I could hear about the night of the ambush. Maybe you or one of the others saw me and saw what I was doing that night or even what happened to me." He exhaled heavily. "I keep thinking if I could only remember what happened that night, then I would know who it is that's after me and why."

"Well, I don't know if I can help you figure out who's

after you, but I do know a group of guys who are going to be over-the-moon happy to see you again." Colton pulled out his cell phone. "And together we'll figure this all out. Don't worry, buddy. You're not alone anymore."

Marcus could not explain the weight he felt lifting off his shoulders at Colton's words.

"Looks like you've been in a firefight," Laura stated, dabbing antibiotic cream on a cut on Bethany's face. It stung, but it was the least of her worries tonight. She was just thankful to be out of the hospital and at Colton and Laura's farmhouse.

Laura stood and closed the first-aid kit. "I'll let you get cleaned up. There are towels in the cabinet in the bathroom if you want to take a shower."

Bethany watched her leave then went into the bathroom and turned on the water, letting it warm. She sat on the edge of the tub and pulled the ponytail from her hair, letting it cascade down her back. She rubbed her face as the events of the day caught up with her. They'd come so close to being killed it made her shudder. Marcus had been her rock and she appreciated him. Because of him, they'd made it to the Blackwell ranch.

Her first instinct was to thank God that they had made it safely, but as she rubbed her shoulder she rethought it. Could she actually claim they had made it safely? They'd been shot at, beaten up and she'd been hit by a car. But they *had* made it to the Blackwell farm and Colton had agreed to phone the other surviving rangers for Marcus to speak with. They were so close to finding out the answers they'd been searching for.

She couldn't call that anything but God's guidance.

Bethany finished her shower, dressed and went downstairs. Colton was showing Marcus—who looked like he'd also cleaned up—his weapons locker and Marcus was trying out the scope of a new, sleek rifle. Bethany helped herself to a handgun and three full rounds. Only as she loaded it and readied it to go did she realize they were all watching her.

"What?" she asked. "I'm a federal agent. I think I can handle this little gun."

Marcus flashed her an easygoing grin. "I'm not sure you'll be able to withstand the jolt of that gun with your shoulder hurt."

She didn't care. "I'll deal with that when the time comes," she retorted. If she needed a weapon, the pain in her shoulder would likely be the least of her worries.

Colton chuckled then moved on with the conversation. "I spoke with each of the fellas. They'll all be here by late afternoon."

"How can they get here so soon?" Bethany asked. "Don't they have jobs and families?"

"They do but when you hear that a teammate you thought was dead is alive, let's just say they had no problem dropping whatever they were doing and hitting the road." He cleared his throat. "We should take the truck and pull your vehicle out of the ravine."

"Good idea," Marcus said.

Colton picked up a rifle then stopped and gave Laura a long kiss goodbye before walking out.

Marcus turned to her and Bethany's heart fluttered. Was he about to kiss her that way? His eyes confirmed he wanted to as he stared into hers and Bethany wasn't sure she would even attempt to stop him.

He put his hand on her cheek and instead only caressed her face. "Get some rest," he whispered to her before he followed Colton outside.

She watched with Laura as the two men climbed into Colton's truck and headed off.

"How long have you two been together?" she asked.

Bethany felt her face warm at that question. "We… we're not in love," she said, a protest that caused Laura to look at her and chuckle.

"Are you sure? Cause I've seen love before and that man loves you."

She did not want to believe Marcus's affections for her were so obvious that even a total stranger could see it, but that was the rub. To Marcus, she was the total stranger. Even if she told him today about how they'd met and their whirlwind romance, it would never be the same for them. It couldn't be. Tears pressed into her eyes and she pushed them back. Maybe if they'd had the time and opportunity to grow their relationship, they might have wound up with a love like the one she saw between Laura and Colton. But they hadn't. They'd been robbed of their only opportunity for a real relationship.

"Why don't you go upstairs and get some rest?" Laura suggested gently. "I'll check on you periodically. I have a feeling that once all the men arrive, it's going to be a long night."

She agreed, thankful for the opportunity to retreat to her room and compose herself.

As she stood at the window and looked out at the

rolling green fields, she admitted the truth. She was on edge not because of her injuries or her unresolved feelings toward Marcus. She loved him. There, she'd admitted it. She loved him. She only hoped she wasn't wasting her emotions on a man who'd betrayed his country.

EIGHT

She waited on the steps of the front porch until the men returned, towing the pickup truck behind Colton's truck. It was a mess, the cab ceiling crushed from the impact of rolling and the front end damaged. It was amazing to her that neither of them had been seriously injured in that crash.

Marcus walked over and sat once they had it unloaded. He had something in his hand and showed it to her. A small, square box with wires she recognized as a tracking device.

"We found it on the pickup. He couldn't have known we would take the truck back in Little Falls so he must have planted it in Waco. That's how he found us."

She pushed a weary hand through her hair. Chalk up another one for the sniper.

"How are you feeling?"

She sighed, frustrated with the whole situation. "You have to stop worrying about me so much. I'm fine."

"I can't help worrying. You're important to me, Bethany."

"I don't want to be important to you." Although, deep down, she wanted to believe in him, longed to believe in him, and could not even imagine that he was ever so heartless as to do the things she'd thought of him. He was a kind, decent man with a protective nature. She could not have been so wrong about him...could she?

Her mind told her she'd been blinded by emotion and attraction. But she had seen him with his men, she had witnessed him with the locals, playing with the kids and being kind to the townspeople. This was just all so confusing because it wasn't adding up. Either he was some kind of Jekyll and Hyde personality or something was very wrong about this entire situation. She was beginning to wonder.

"Tell me again about the people who cared for you. What exactly did they say to make you go into hiding?"

He leaned back. "Well, I didn't speak the language. I knew a few words and phrases and their English was broken at best. It was more the fear that I felt in them. They were frightened when troops came by. It seemed like they were looking for something or someone. The family kept saying, 'CIA bad. Hide, hide. CIA danger.' That led me to believe that the CIA was after me for some reason and I couldn't remember why or what I'd done. I thought my life was in danger, so I did as they told me and I hid."

"It seems they were right. Someone in the CIA was after you, probably wanting to make certain you hadn't survived. But you don't remember seeing anyone?"

He shook his head. "Not anyone I could identify. I heard the threats, though. I heard them threaten to burn down the village if they discovered the villagers were harboring an American fugitive. I thought I was that fugitive they were referring to. I thought I'd done something terrible to have the CIA after me. So I hid. But the not knowing has been eating away at me. I had to know. I knew whatever it was, I had to come and face it."

Marcus reached out, took her hand and sighed. "I don't know how to prove to you that I'm not what you think I am," he declared. "If you're looking for a pile of evidence that says I'm not involved…well, you may not get that. I'm glad we're here and I'm hoping for answers, but I also know I may not find them. Eventually you may have to decide either to trust me or not to trust me."

Bethany shook her head. "I don't know how to do that." She wanted to trust Marcus. She wanted to believe that he was not involved in selling secrets to the enemy. But her mind kept floating back to the way she'd been hurt and the rip of betrayals when she'd realized Marcus was still alive.

He stood and forced her to her feet. Her gaze was downcast and she refused to make eye contact. He touched her face, caressing her cheek. "I don't know how to reassure you. You know me now. You know my heart. I cannot believe that I could do the things you're accusing me of. I know in my heart I wasn't a part of it. I couldn't have been."

She raised her head and looked at him, wanting to melt into his embrace and wishing she could be as certain. But mostly she wanted to know how he could be so calm when she was terrified about what they might find out when the other rangers arrived.

"I don't understand how you can have such faith in a God that is leading you to prison and possibly death. Treason still carries the death penalty."

He took a deep breath and she saw that he was trying to find the words to help her understand. "I made choices in my life, Bethany. It's those choices that are leading me where I'm going. God didn't force me to make the decisions I've made. He's only helping me to find out the truth about myself. How can I ever repent if I don't even know what I've done? And, if I did do those terrible things, then those were my choices, not His. I have faith that, no matter what I discover about myself, God can use it for His purpose. That's all I really know."

Bethany turned and stomped off. She still did not have the truth of the matter and she needed a clear sign.

He moved toward her and when he wrapped his arms around her, she found herself leaning into his embrace.

"I *am* scared," he admitted. "I don't want to find out I'm a bad guy. I don't want to know that I'm responsible for costing men their lives. But no matter what I find out, no one can ever say that what I feel for you now isn't real. I know we had something, Beth, and I know you aren't ready to go there, but I do care for you. I can't explain how I've only known you a short time and I feel so completely taken by you."

She closed her eyes, fighting every urge to tell him the truth about their whirlwind romance and how much he'd come to mean to her. Instead she broke from his embrace and went inside.

Alone in her room, she let the tears fall because she still didn't know if what they'd shared before was real or just a ploy to ply her for government secrets.

Levi Thompson appeared at the farm first in the early afternoon, several hours before the others were scheduled to arrive. He'd been close by, in New Orleans, meeting with a neurologist he hoped could help him with the debilitating back pains he still suffered from the ambush. Levi had been hurt the worst of the survivors. He was also the man Garrett had pulled to safety instead of Marcus.

Marcus checked the men off one by one, remembering their names and referencing the group photo that hung on Colton's wall.

Matt Ross, the tall and thin commander of the group, now worked for the DEA.

Josh Adams, an easygoing weapons expert, had married the FBI agent who'd taken down a human trafficking ring and rescued his niece from its grasp.

Blake Michaels, the former tactical officer who'd just recently dismantled a corrupt government in Arkansas and recently taken over as its sheriff.

Garrett Lewis, Marcus's supposed best friend, was the kill-shot sniper who'd rescued his secret son from a kidnapper and pulled Levi Thompson to safety the night of the ambush.

Garrett seemed most shocked by Marcus's appearance and stared at him in awe for several moments before pushing the others out of the way and pulling Marcus into a bear hug.

"I can't believe it's you," he whispered. "I'm so thankful you're alive."

"Yeah, how exactly is that possible?" Matt asked.

"And where have you been all this time?" Blake demanded.

He told them the story, leaving nothing out about his amnesia, including being hunted by a rogue CIA agent and the attack on him and Bethany that had led them to find Colton.

He saw their stunned faces and knew they were all having trouble processing it. Finally, Matt spoke up. "That's something, Marcus. I wish I could help you, but I didn't see anything that might clear this up."

Each of the others shared his sentiments. Only Levi didn't respond. Marcus looked at him. "What about you, Levi? Did you see something?"

He shook his head slowly. "I'm sorry, Marcus. I thankfully didn't lose all my memories like you did, but everything from that night and even a couple prior to it are gone. I don't remember anything that happened."

Disappointment coursed through Marcus. He had hoped for answers tonight but it seemed no one had any.

"What's going to happen to you now?" Josh asked him.

Marcus realized he hadn't really thought that far ahead. "I guess I'll go back to Langley with Bethany. I'm told the CIA have ways to help me remember."

"I don't trust the CIA," Colton told him. "You may just disappear again."

He nodded. "I've considered that. I don't really trust them, either, but I trust Bethany. She won't let anything happen to me."

"And what if she can't stop it?" Josh asked.

"Then she'll find me. She's already done it once. She'll find me again."

"She won't have to do it alone this time," Garrett assured him. "We're not letting you go, either."

They all nodded, echoing Garrett's sentiment. The camaraderie he felt for these men was instinctual and it gave him a good feeling of not being on his own anymore.

As the group began to disperse, Garrett pulled Marcus aside. His face was flushed and he looked anxious. "I owe you an apology."

Marcus saw where this was going. Guilt was eating away at this man. "No, you don't."

"I do. I left you there. I had you in my sights, Marcus. I could have sworn you were gone. You were so still and lifeless. Maybe if I'd gotten closer to you, it would have made a difference…"

"You did what you thought was right," Marcus told him gruffly. "I don't blame you. If you'd acted differently then Levi might have been the one to die that night."

Garrett raked a hand through his hair. "I just can't get over it. You lost two years of your life. I feel responsible. And, Bethany, I should have known she would be the one to find you. That lady was always a spitfire. She really fell hard for you, Marcus."

Marcus grabbed hold of his meaning and stood. "What do you mean?"

"The two of you hardly spent a moment apart that you weren't working or sleeping."

He slid back down to his seat as Garrett's words sank in to him. He and Bethany had been together, after all. Why had she denied it for so long?

Because you hurt her, that's why.

He rubbed his face then thanked Garrett and walked away. He had to talk to her now before he lost his nerve or let one more moment pass without sweeping her into his arms and telling her how much he cared for her.

He found her in the barn. She had set up a target and was practicing with the gun she'd gotten from Colton. Just as he'd thought, she was having trouble with that shoulder. He walked up and grabbed her from behind, spinning her to face him.

"You really shouldn't sneak up on someone brandishing a firearm," she told him, her voice choked and her breath thready as he closed the distance between them.

"Even if I really need to kiss you and I can't wait another moment to do it?"

She stared at him dumbfounded. Finally she dropped the gun. "Oh, then, yeah, that's okay."

He swept her into his arms, his lips finding hers in a kiss that seemed to reverberate through his memories like a tidal wave.

She pulled away from him, her heart pounding so hard he could feel it against his chest "You found the photograph on your phone?"

He shook his head, unsure of what she was referring to. "What photograph? What phone?"

Her face flushed, but she shook her head and pulled him close. "Never mind that. Kiss me again."

He couldn't stop the grin that spread across his face at her command. "Yes, ma'am."

I have the answers you seek. Meet me in the barn.

Marcus found the note lying on his bed when he went upstairs. The memory of that kiss and the way Bethany had responded to him had been on his mind all night and he hadn't even been able to concentrate on the stories his teammates were sharing.

Excitement bubbled up inside him at finding the note. He didn't recognize the handwriting, but he was thrilled at the prospect that someone in the house had answers for him. But why all the secrecy? Why didn't they just come out and tell him the truth?

He slipped on his jacket and walked down the stairs. Hearing laughter, he smiled, recognizing Bethany's laughter in the mix as she sat at the table and listened to the stories. She was becoming so important to him and he was happy she was having moments of joy in a dire situation.

He kept walking and headed outside to the barn. A part of him knew he should tell Bethany about finding the note, but he'd hesitated before making the decision to go without her. It wasn't that he wanted to intentionally deceive her; he was just scared of what he might learn when he met the note writer. The secret nature of it made him nervous. Was he about to hear something about himself he wouldn't like? Was it possible this mystery person was about to confirm his worst fears— that he wasn't good enough for someone like Bethany?

The thought that this might be a trap by the sniper briefly ran through his mind, causing him to wonder if he should bring a gun. He chose not to, deciding it was unlikely the sniper could get that note into the house with everyone around without being seen. Someone already here must have left it for him, someone who knew what had happened to him the night of the ambush.

He drew a deep breath then walked inside the barn. "Hello?" he called when no one appeared. He heard nothing but the sounds of the animals in the stalls. He reached out and stroked a horse's nose. "Who's here, girl? I know you didn't write that note, did you?"

The horse whinnied and Marcus stroked her again.

"I wrote it."

Marcus turned at the sound of the voice. He didn't recognize it and, when he turned, he didn't know the man who appeared from behind a corner, either.

The guy was shorter than Marcus, but fit. His short hair was slicked back and shone as much as his pressed slacks and shiny shoes. He removed the sunglasses from his face.

Marcus searched his brain for some slither of recognition but there was nothing. "Who are you?" he asked, moving away from the horse.

"My name is Dillon Montgomery. I'm a Special Agent with the CIA, covert operations."

The CIA? Had Bethany finally given up on letting him discover the truth about himself and called in reinforcements to bring him in? He could not blame her after all they'd been through. But if she'd thought he would run, she was wrong. He had made her a promise to go in freely if his quest for answers didn't pan out and he intended to keep his word.

"How did you know where to find me? And why haven't I seen you here before?"

"It's part of my job to get in and out of places unnoticed. As for how I knew where you were, I've been following Bethany's investigation. What happened to you, Marcus? We all thought you'd died in the ambush."

"So I've heard. How do you know me?"

"We worked together overseas," Dillon answered.

"Did I handle protection for you?"

He chuckled. "No, nothing like that. You were doing work for me, actually."

"What kind of work?" Marcus demanded.

"You were in a dangerous job and not making a lot of money doing it. I helped you out in that aspect."

He didn't like the dodgy way Dillon was avoiding coming right out and telling him how they knew one another. "How exactly did you do that?"

"You see, I have this operation going. You and others like you tell me things about certain operations and in return you're well compensated."

Marcus's heart dropped. Dillon was the rogue agent Bethany's boss had warned her about. The one recruiting US soldiers to sell secrets to the enemy. Now Dillon was telling Marcus that he was one of those soldiers. Dread trickled through him. He was a traitor. He'd betrayed his country, sold secrets to the enemy. He was the worst of the worst. No wonder he'd tried so hard to run away from his past. He rubbed his head, wishing he could go back and un-learn this about himself.

"I'm a traitor."

"Don't get so caught up in labels. You're doing your duty fighting for your country and, in return, the big wigs of America are getting filthy, stinking rich off this war against terror." Dillon smirked. "Why shouldn't the men and women on the front lines who are carrying the weight of the fighting get something, too? It's only fair. I'm only trying to level the playing field."

"And how many soldiers have died because of the information you've been handing over to the enemy? No, I refuse to believe I was ever part of that."

"It's true, Marcus. You were one of my best soldiers. When I thought you'd died, I lost a good man. I tried searching for you in the hope that you'd survived somehow, but I wasn't able to find you. I wondered why you were hiding from me."

"You were the one who was trying to kill me."

Dillon shrugged. "I confess when I learned you were alive, I thought you meant to betray me, so I tried to have you killed. I didn't believe the amnesia story at first, but now I've changed my mind about you. Now, I realize the amnesia had you confused. I am glad you're alive."

Marcus hated what he was hearing about himself. His head was spinning. What was his next move? The biggest thing on his mind was how in the world he was going to tell Bethany what he'd learned. Hearing the truth about his past also meant realizing that he'd lost any chance for a future with Bethany.

"I want you back, Marcus," Dillon continued. "Your contributions were undeniable. You were a big asset to my operation and no one could recruit new members like you could."

Every word the other man spoke just made the ugliness of what Marcus had done worse. Not only had he sold secrets, he had talked other men, fellow soldiers, into doing the same. He felt sick at the idea.

"Stop," Marcus demanded. "I don't want to hear any more."

"You don't have a choice. You need to come with me now. You and I both know Bethany will never understand this. She'll have you in cuffs and marching back to Langley in a hot minute and you'll spend the rest of your life either in prison or in facing the death penalty. I know that's not what you want."

"Maybe it's what I deserve."

Dillon sighed. "You're not thinking clearly, Marcus. You're confused. Come with me now. Give yourself some time to process all this before you let Bethany lead you into a circus of bureaucracy. Don't let your fate rest in political decisions."

Anger simmered inside him. It was bad enough he'd done such despicable things, but to compound that by running away, going back into hiding and continuing to betray his country was unconscionable. He could not even fathom a situation where he'd done such things, but he admitted he had no idea what kind of person he used to be.

He started to tell Dillon he would not go with him. If he'd committed these terrible deeds, then he needed to confront his past and accept his consequences. However, before he could speak, fear gripped him. Dillon was right. He was putting his life into the hands of an agency that operated in secret and meted out justice in the same way. Would he be given a fair trial? Or would he vanish without a trace and Marcus Allen would remain the soldier who'd died the night of the ambush?

He hated the indecision that pricked at him. He knew the right thing to do. He just didn't know if he could do it. He knew only one thing for certain.

He'd lost Bethany.

Bethany was sitting on the porch enjoying the cool night air and admiring the clear sky. It was so beautiful here and peaceful. How long had it been since she'd experienced such peace? Too long.

From inside, she could hear the men around the table sharing war stories back and forth and imagined Marcus was soaking them all up. She hoped it would help spark some sort of memory for him.

She was under no illusion that the reason for her peaceful attitude was due to anything other than that amazing kiss she and Marcus had shared. She'd spent years remembering the feel of his lips on hers and it was just as incredible now as it had been back then.

The front door opened and someone stepped out. She expected it would be Marcus but it wasn't.

Instead Levi walked outside and glanced up at the night sky. "It's beautiful here, isn't it?"

"Yes, it is. What's going on in there?"

"You know, just telling tales." He gave her a sly grin and shrugged. "It's what we do." Then he gave her a long, cold look. "You were there, weren't you? I remember you being there the days before the ambush."

"Yes, I was there. My partner, Dillon, and I were working on logistics for the operation."

"You found the translator, didn't you?"

His tone had turned cold and she swallowed hard before answering. She had a feeling she knew where this conversation was heading. "Yes, I did find him. I thought he seemed like a good man."

"He wasn't." Levi spun to her, his face twisted and hard. "He led most of my team to their deaths. You're responsible for that."

Her instinct was to match his hard tone with each angry syllable, but she didn't. Instead she stood. "I think I'll take a walk." She slid by him and off the porch, but he wasn't finished with their conversation.

Panic pulsed through her. She hadn't even considered that these men might blame her for the ambush. They didn't know what she knew...that the translator she'd hired was most likely a patsy for a more threatening figure.

She heard his footsteps as he followed her off the porch. "How can you sleep at night?" Levi demanded. "How can you sleep knowing how many people you've killed?"

She stopped and turned to him. If he would allow her to explain, he might understand that she wasn't to blame, but she could see he was in no mood to listen.

His opinion of her was set in concrete and wouldn't be budged.

"I'm going back inside," she said, trying to move past him, but he grabbed her arm to stop her.

"You don't get away that easily." He grit the words out.

"Let me go," she said, trying to jerk her arm from his grasp. "You have no idea what you're talking about. You don't know me or what happened."

Then she saw it…the bandage on his arm as he held her. Her breath caught in her throat. That bandage was low on his arm, near the wrist…the same location where she'd sliced open the attacker's arm with a meat thermometer back at the Allen house.

He followed her gaze to his bandage and his face softened in an effect that didn't quite reach his eyes. "I cut myself shaving," he told her in an excuse that was so ridiculous it couldn't possibly be true. He grabbed her other arm and pulled her to him, his tone changing to a sneer. "Actually, I had a little accident in the kitchen. Someone needs to learn how to use kitchen utensils."

"Oh, I'm a whiz in the kitchen." She hardened her stare and locked eyes with him. "Let me go now."

"That's not going to happen," he told her. "First, I need you to hear something."

Levi spun her around and clamped his hand over her mouth, pinning her arms with his. Then, yanking her against him, he dragged her away from the house.

She struggled violently but her shoulder was still sore and he had her locked in a hold she could not break free from. She tried to scream for help, but even her cries were silenced by his hand over her mouth.

Fear rushed through her. Levi, one of Marcus's fellow rangers, was the sniper who'd been trying to kill them. And now they'd come right to him. Were the other rangers part of this, as well, or was Levi working alone? It seemed unlikely. He must have had help to pull this off, but who else was involved?

He dragged her toward the barn and Bethany heard voices coming from inside. Levi pressed himself against the wall so they would not be seen.

"Be quiet and listen," he ordered.

But she didn't take orders from him. She continued to struggle, worry seeping into her mind at what he would do to her now that she knew his true identity. However, she stopped fighting when a familiar voice reached her ears.

Marcus!

She tried to pull away and call for help from Marcus, but Levi once again blocked her attempt.

"Hush and listen," he hissed in a quiet but firm command.

She had little choice. The voices were muffled, but what she heard made her heart grow cold.

"I don't want to go to jail," Marcus was telling someone. "If I go with you, what happens to Bethany?"

Another male voice answered. She couldn't place it, but it sounded oddly familiar. "She'll be fine. The entire Agency knows she's been obsessed with finding you. It won't be difficult to convince everyone that the man she thought was you, was actually an imposter and she made up the whole 'being chased' incidents."

She gasped. Whoever was speaking worked for the CIA and had the means to spread lies about her within it. Was this the rogue CIA agent Rick had warned her about? And, if he was speaking to Marcus, trying to convince him to go with him, did that mean Marcus had worked for him all along?

"But my mother and sister. They've seen me. So have all these men here."

"A grieving family will believe anything. Cons prey on them all the time. We can spin it that way. And I'm not sure any of these guys are actually convinced it's you. They're playing along in case you're the real deal, but you can't forget they've been living with the fallout of your death for years."

"I can't do that to her. I won't."

"Don't worry, Marcus. Her reputation will take some hits but nothing will happen to her. At the worst, she leaves the Agency in disgrace. That's still better than having to watch you be executed for treason, isn't it? I'm leaving this place in ten minutes. Be ready to go or stay and face the consequences of your choices."

Anger and betrayal ripped through her. She finally knew the truth about Marcus. He had been working for the enemy. Her heart ripped into pieces and only anger kept her standing when she wanted to fall apart.

She was thankful Levi had brought her here. He had helped her find the answers she'd needed, but now her mind spun at the contradiction of it all. If Levi was try-ing to help her discover who Marcus really was, then why had he been trying to kill them all this time? She could almost make herself believe he'd been trying to bring down only Marcus if there hadn't been so many collateral victims in the process. He'd murdered Milo and Marie and tried to kill Elizabeth and Shannon along with her and Marcus. How could he ever justify those actions?

Pulling away from Levi, she ran into the barn to confront Marcus not only about his deeds but also about the fact that he was considering running out on her, allowing her to be made a fool of. She gasped when she saw the familiar face of the man Marcus was talking to.

Dillon Montgomery. Her former partner. The man who had tried to win her heart. The man who had told her it was time to get over Marcus once and for all.

The rogue CIA agent recruiting soldiers for the enemy.

Her heart fell as she realized she'd once again been betrayed by another man she'd trusted.

NINE

Marcus couldn't do it. He might have been a traitor to his country at one time, but he would not go back to that life now. He was about to tell Dillon he didn't want any part of his outfit when a sound behind him grabbed his attention.

He turned to see Bethany standing in the doorway, her jaw set firm and her eyes blazing. His first thought was to wonder how much she'd overheard, but her stance and glare told him all he needed to know. She'd heard everything. Dillon had spilled the sordid details of Marcus's past and Bethany had listened to every word. Now, they both knew the truth about him.

She headed toward him and he was ready to explain, but then he realized she was marching toward Dillon. He stood firm and gave her a smirk as she approached him.

"Good to see you again, Bethany. How are you?"

"Dillon Montgomery. I can't believe it's you. You're the one behind all of this."

"Grow up, Bethany. The world is bigger than that little cubicle you work in."

"You sicken me."

She turned to Marcus and he saw disgust in her face. She shook her head. "I can't even look at you, Marcus."

He reached for her arm. "Please, let me explain."

She jerked away. "Don't touch me."

Shame filled him. "I don't know what to say. I didn't expect this."

"I made a mistake trusting you, Marcus. I should have gone with my original thought and not gotten sucked into your fantasy that you were the good guy." Tears filled her eyes. "You did it to me again. You made me trust you." She turned to Dillon, then back to Marcus. "I'm calling for backup then I'm taking you both back to Langley to face prosecution."

"You don't really think I'm just going to let you walk away, do you?" Dillon said to her. He pulled a gun from his jacket and aimed it at them.

She turned and glared at Dillon. "Try and stop me."

She started for the door when someone from outside filled the doorway. She stopped. Levi stood there, blocking her path, a rifle laying in his arms.

Dillon's next words cleared up Levi's presence. "I think you both know my associate."

"So this is your attack dog, is it?" Bethany looked at Levi. "I knew you were involved when I spotted that wound on your arm. I hope it hurt when I jammed that meat thermometer into your arm."

He sneered at her. "I knew at that moment that I was going to enjoy killing you."

Dillon stepped forward. "Back down, Levi. No one is going to kill anyone. At least, that's not my intent, not anymore. As I said before, when I thought you were going to betray me, I made sure Levi was tracking Bethany's investigation. He had orders to kill you on site, but unfortunately, his injuries sustained in the ambush have affected his abilities as a sniper. He wasn't able to complete the job, which is a fortunate turn for us both."

Levi gave a low growl, obviously not enjoying Dillon's pointing out his failures.

"What do you want from us?" Marcus demanded.

"I want you, Marcus. You're the reason I'm here. You come with me now and I promise you Bethany won't be harmed."

"If you think I'm just going to look the other way, then you're crazy," she countered. "I'm taking you down, Dillon."

Levi tried to grab her but Marcus stepped in front of her. He didn't have his gun on him, but he would fight for her with his last breath. "Don't you touch her," he warned him.

Dillon attacked him from behind, kicking out the backs of his legs and sending him to his knees. Before Marcus could even turn, he felt a sting on the back of his neck. A rush of warmth flowed through him and he doubled over as dizziness overtook him. Bethany screamed and, through a haze, he saw Dillon grab her. She kicked and fought him, but she was no match for both him and Levi. Dillon pulled out a syringe and shoved it into her neck while Levi held her down. After a moment, she stopped struggling. That must have been what they'd done to him too. They'd drugged them both.

God, please help me save her.

He resisted the urge to pass out and gathered what little strength he could muster to lunge at Dillon, who only laughed as he moved out of the way. Marcus hit the ground. He lunged again, grunting at the effort, but he couldn't let him take Bethany.

"Leave her alone."

His vision began to fade but he saw a car pull up to the barn. Dillon picked up Bethany and carried her to the car, where Levi helped him load her into the back seat.

Dillon returned and knelt beside Marcus. "I hope you remember this when you wake. Meet me at the old drive-in theater. Come alone if you want to see Bethany alive again." He stood and walked to the car.

"Don't," Marcus cried as Dillon slid into the passenger's seat and the car roared away.

Marcus's heart fell as it disappeared from view. He had to get up. He had to catch up with them. He had to get help.

His vision dimmed and he felt himself fall. Just before he lost consciousness, dread filled him. He had to save Bethany.

Marcus came to, his head pounding. He pulled himself to his feet, having no idea how long he had been out, but the sky outside the barn doors was still dark. Every single moment he'd lost was one that put Bethany in greater danger. He couldn't believe he'd let Dillon ambush him like that. They must have planned it that way. Dillon would attack while they were focused on Levi.

Levi.

He had to get to the other rangers and let them know one of their own was crooked. Mostly, he had to beg for their help. He couldn't rescue Bethany on his own. Dillon's words about the rangers not truly believing it was him came flooding back. Was he right about them? And if they thought he was lying, would they want to help someone who was accusing one of their own of treason?

He crossed the yard and burst into the house, shouting for help. A figure on the couch lifted up. Garrett. A moment later the others came rushing down the stairs.

"What's going on?" Colton asked. Behind him on the stairs were Matt, Josh and Blake, all looking as if he'd wakened them from a sound sleep.

"Where's Levi?" Marcus demanded.

"He left," Blake told him. "He had to get back to New Orleans for an appointment in the morning."

Marcus stared at them all. Would they believe him about Levi? He couldn't worry about their feelings on the matter. "No, he didn't. He and Dillon Montgomery just kidnapped Bethany."

They all looked at him, confused. Garrett rubbed his eyes as if trying to clear out the sleep. "What? Who is Dillon Montgomery?"

"He's CIA. He was there the night of the ambush."

Josh stepped forward. "Yeah, he was working with Bethany, wasn't he?"

"He was supposed to be working with her. In truth, he was working for himself. He was recruiting soldiers to work for the enemy. I believe he was the one who leaked the information about our mission that night."

Again, they all looked confused at his accusation. Colton stepped forward. "And you're claiming that Levi is working with him? That's some accusation, Marcus."

"It's the truth. They attacked us in the barn. Levi grabbed Bethany and Dillon told me if I wanted to see her alive again then I had to come alone to the old drive-in theater."

"Sounds like a trap," Matt stated.

Marcus nodded. "I know. That's why I need your help."

They all looked stunned and Marcus wondered once again if they would believe his tale. These men had two years of bonding among them and Marcus was the outsider. Maybe they had once been his friends and teammates, but he didn't even remember them. How could he expect them to trust him against one of their own?

Marcus waited for someone to speak to give him some sense of what was on their minds. His was already working through plans to rescue Bethany on his own if need be. Whatever they said, whether they believed him or called him a liar, he was going after her. Even if she never wanted to see him again, he was going to make certain she was safe.

Finally, Colton moved. He grabbed his phone and started dialing. "I'm calling Levi."

Garrett stood. "I'll get dressed."

He and the others disappeared upstairs and Marcus still had no idea whether or not they believed him.

Marcus rushed to the weapons locker and opened it.

He would need serious firepower to defeat Dillon and Levi. Even then, without the help of the rangers, he did not know how he could save her.

He fell into a chair as the hopelessness of the situation leveled him. She was in this situation because of him, because of his past. How could he have betrayed everything he'd joined the military to fight for? He didn't understand it. Bowing his head, he buried his face in his hands. He'd been so certain that when the truth was uncovered, he would find that this had all been an enormous mistake.

He lifted his head. "I can't do this alone," he whispered. He needed the help of the rangers to rescue Bethany and bring Dillon and Levi to justice. It didn't matter that he didn't deserve their help. All that mattered was Bethany, and he would do anything it took to bring her through this safely.

Please, God, please keep her safe.

Suddenly, Garrett appeared in the doorway and pushed past Marcus to reach for a weapon.

Marcus stared at him. "Does this mean you believe me?"

Garrett sighed. "Honestly, I'm not sure, but that doesn't mean I'm going to let you walk into an ambush without backup."

He followed Garrett into the kitchen. The guys had a map spread out on the table, and Matt and Blake were poring over it while the others were gearing up.

"Our first move should be to scope out the drive-in. What do we know about it?" Matt asked.

Blake spoke up. "Colton and I are familiar with it.

It's been abandoned for years. But our one advantage is probably that we know this area better than they do. Laura was kidnapped and held there last year. Only two buildings are still standing and we blew out the door to the projector room to rescue her." He rubbed a hand along his jaw. "That means they would have to be holed up inside the concession building. It's long and narrow, but there are a lot of rooms, including an old freezer, where they could be hiding."

Colton moved to look at the aerial map. "We should assume that if he's not working alone he'll have a sniper perched somewhere high, probably on the frame of the old screen."

"Agreed," Matt said. "Someone will have to take him out."

Josh stepped forward. "I'll do it."

"No," Matt said. "Garrett is the best shot." He looked at Garrett. "Take out whoever is up there then take his place. We may need our own sniper before this is over."

Garrett nodded, but Marcus noticed how not one of them mentioned Levi by name. Was it because they still weren't convinced it was him? It didn't matter. As long as they were there, they would learn the truth on their own.

"We'll take three trucks. Me, Josh and Colton will enter through the east side and find our positions. Garrett, you and Blake get on the scaffold and take out that sniper." Matt looked at Marcus. "You'll go in alone just as they told you to."

"Do you think they'll believe I'm alone?"

"Not if they're smart. They'll know you would never

come alone, but maybe they have actually convinced themselves we wouldn't help you."

That was the very thing Dillon had warned him about and, in this respect, he was glad Dillon had been wrong. They might not completely trust him, but they were going to help him rescue Bethany.

"There's something else," Marcus said. He hoped it wouldn't affect their decision to help, but he knew he couldn't pull them into this battle without telling them the truth. "I came here searching for answers about my past. Well, Dillon told me I was working for him, selling secrets to the enemy. He claims I was one of the soldiers he recruited. I thought you all should know before you risk your lives for me." He glanced at each of their faces expecting revulsion and an immediate walkout, but they didn't.

Colton looked at him. "Listen, this guy Dillon sounds like bad news. How do you even know you can believe what he says? Maybe he was lying."

Marcus hadn't considered that. Was it possible he had only been trying to lure Marcus in when he'd told him he was a traitor? If he'd really only wanted to kill Marcus, he'd had his opportunity in the barn.

Josh spoke up, too. "I honestly don't know what I believe. I have a tough time believing what you've said about Levi. I've known him for years and I never would have believed this. It's possible he's involved. It's possible you both were involved with this CIA guy. I just don't know. What I do know is that there are some situations you can't wait around to find out all the details about. You just have to act."

Matt nodded but added a warning. "Rest assured, if we find out you were involved in any kind of treachery, we will take you out, too."

Marcus couldn't blame them. They were cautious but still willing to help. He breathed a sigh of relief. He might not be able to escape the consequences of his past choices, but hopefully Bethany wouldn't have to pay for them.

The cold concrete was the first thing Bethany was aware of as she slipped into consciousness. She lifted her head and immediately groaned at the pain. She was suddenly aware that someone else was with her. And then the entire situation came rushing back to her.

She jumped up. Levi was pacing, his gun in hand. He looked jittery and Bethany knew that wasn't a good sign.

"Where are we?" she asked.

"Somewhere safe."

The way he gripped his gun and the wild look in his eyes made Bethany worry. She fumed that she'd even entertained the idea that Levi had been trying to help her. Of course, he'd been leading her into a trap. But she wasn't going to get out of this by calling him names. Now was the time to be smart. He'd probably once been a decent guy. Most people that joined the military and made it all the way to becoming an army ranger were full of patriotism and the idea of justice. Somehow, he had allowed Dillon to get into his head, but she had no clue how that had happened. Nothing she'd uncovered in her investigation would have led her to believe Levi was vulnerable to recruitment.

Maybe if she could get him talking, she could find a way to play on his sensibilities and get out of this mess alive.

"What's the plan here, Levi? What's the exit strategy?"

He glared at her but she continued. "You always have to have an exit plan. How are you going to get out of this? Marcus knows you're the mole now. He's going to tell everyone. Your time is up."

"Marcus knows, but if you think the other rangers are going to believe a word he says then you're crazy. I've spent two years with these men and they'll believe me over him all day long. He's the one who's alone in the world, not me."

Her heart clenched at the thought of losing Marcus, then she remembered that she'd already lost him. He was a traitor, a turncoat, an enemy to his country. And he'd betrayed her. She knew it was the truth now. Still, she could not let him walk into a trap. Surely he wouldn't come alone. But was Levi correct about the others? Would they believe him when he told them how Levi and Dillon had kidnapped her?

Her hands were bound with duct tape. Hard to break so she needed to find something sharp to cut it. She glanced around while Levi was otherwise occupied. Her heart leaped when she spotted something that might work to cut the duct tape. With her back against the wall, she pressed into the railing and rubbed her hands against it.

Levi spun around and saw her. "Stop that!" he shouted, grabbing her and pulling her away from the railing and more toward the center of the room. He dropped her and returned to the window.

So much for that, but she wasn't giving up. She had no fantasy that she was going to make it out of this alive and she was determined, if she was going to die anyway, she wasn't going to go down without a fight.

The door creaked open and Levi spun around, raising his weapon, ready to shoot.

Dillon sauntered inside. "Put that away," he barked at Levi. "One of these days, you'll accidentally shoot me."

He stared at Bethany then knelt beside her, his face close to hers as he gave a smug grin.

She'd never wanted anything more than she wanted to wipe that snide look off his face.

"You gave us a good run, Bethany, but let's face it. You're out of your league."

"You sicken me." She stormed at him. "You're a liar and a traitor to your country."

"I'm a businessman. An entrepreneur. I provide a service and, like any good businessman, I provide it to the highest bidder. Unfortunately, that's never the US government."

"And what about the men you've turned into criminals?" she demanded. "How can you live with yourself?"

"I provide opportunities. I don't force anyone to participate"

"You seek out the vulnerable and trap them into your service. You turn men, good men, into criminals." She scowled at him. "How did you convince Marcus to do your bidding? Nothing I found proves he needed the money. How did you lure him in?"

Dillon flashed her another evil grin then stood. "Marcus?" He laughed. "Do you know what his nickname was among his ranger team? They called him Boy Scout. I never even tried to recruit Marcus. I knew he wouldn't be receptive to my proposal."

She was confused. "Then how—how did he come to work for you?"

"He didn't. He never worked for me."

This revelation thrilled her and devastated her all at once. She'd thought the worst of him and he'd never done anything to deserve it. But that information raised another question. "I don't understand. If he didn't work for you, then why are you trying to kill him? And why did I overhear you tell him he did in the barn?"

"He compromised my operation. He overheard me and Levi talking the night of the ambush, and he figured out what was happening. I couldn't let him go back and tell everyone what he'd heard. You understand I couldn't withstand that kind of spotlight. I had too much at stake to let him walk away. So I shot him, but not before he'd gotten in a few shots of his own. He shot Levi pretty badly. I thought I'd killed him, so you can imagine my shock when you actually found him alive."

Anger burned inside her. "You followed my investigation. You were the one who encouraged me in it."

"Well, I had a vested interest in making sure the man was actually dead, didn't I?"

"Then why—" She fumbled over her words. "Is that

why you started a relationship with me? To use me?" It was the worst kind of betrayal and the same thing she'd accused Marcus of doing to her.

"Well, that wouldn't have lasted much longer if you hadn't found him. I was fairly certain he wasn't coming back and I had plans to tell you things just weren't working out for us when you returned from Texas." He grinned. "It's funny how things work out, isn't it?"

"You could have killed him in the barn. Why didn't you?"

"Because I'd already shot him once and it didn't take." He stood and paced the room like an anxious animal ready to pounce. She had never before seen Dillon so agitated. "When you told me he had amnesia, I thought it was a joke, a ploy on his part. When I realized it was actually true, I saw an opportunity. Sure, I could have just taken him out then and there, but I'm an opportunist, Bethany. If I have to kill Marcus to keep him from spilling his guts and bringing attention to my operation, then I will. But I want more than that."

"*More?* What more can you possibly want from him?"

"I want him to actually get his hands dirty for me." His eyes gleamed with excitement. "Can you imagine it? He's already officially dead, so he can go anywhere and no one will be looking for him. I can use a man like that in my operation. If I can convince him to work just one operation with me, then I'll own him. He'll have too much to lose if he goes to the Feds. He'll be forced to work with me."

"And how do you think you're going to accomplish that?"

"You are the answer. Marcus will do whatever I tell him to do in order to keep you safe. You are my bargaining chip, Bethany. He'll do whatever I command as long as it saves your life."

She glared at him. "I'm not foolish enough to believe you're going to allow me to live and neither is Marcus. We both know your identity now."

He flashed her a long, sly grin. "I knew you were smart, Bethany, but you'd be amazed what the power of fear can do. He might not do it to save his own life, but to save yours, he just might."

She pulled at the binding on her hands and understood his meaning. No one was getting out of this alive.

Marcus turned onto the dirt road that led him to the old drive-in. His hands tightened against the steering wheel as he passed the boarded-up ticket booth. He wasn't alone and he knew it. But that didn't still the apprehension that gripped him at the thought of what Bethany might be going through. If Dillon or Levi had hurt her, he didn't know how he would control himself.

A voice in the earpiece calmed him. "Rangers, are we all in position?" Matt's calm, commanding voice seemed familiar and the responses to his shout-out reassured Marcus that despite his own lack of knowledge of them, his instincts were correct that he could trust these men.

"In position," Colton responded.

"I'm here," Josh said.

Marcus felt better hearing their voices and knowing he didn't have to face this alone. Of course, Marcus knew he wasn't really alone and never had been. He'd had God on his side all the time he'd trekked through Afghanistan and Iran and all the way back to the US. It was a marvel that he'd made that journey without incident. Without God on his side, he would likely be sitting in an Iranian prison, a captive, or more likely dead.

Finally, Blake's voice sounded in his earpiece. "We're here, too." Then, after a moment's hesitation, he stated, "No one is here. There's no sniper's nest."

There was a moment of silence when Marcus was certain they would all decide he was crazy or lying and would pack up and leave. But a second or two later, Matt came back on the headset. "Take your position and be on the lookout."

Marcus let out the anxious breath he'd been holding and gripped the steering wheel again, thankful they were still there.

He wasn't leaving here without her.

"Report your condition," Matt stated again.

Each man came back with an answer of "All clear."

"I have eyes on the entire area," Garrett stated. "I have zero enemy visibility."

Levi wasn't showing himself, but Marcus felt in his gut that he was out there somewhere and would eventually appear.

The dirt road opened onto a cleared lot with two buildings. One was an old shed with the front part of it partially blasted away. Blake had told him about how they'd blasted it open in an effort to save Laura, who'd been trapped inside with a madman. The other building was a long concrete structure that looked to still be intact. He could see from the front that it had once housed the concession stand. Glimpsing an SUV parked on the far side, he pulled up beside it and stopped.

"Don't worry," Garrett's voice said in his ear. "I disabled the SUV. They won't be going anywhere in that vehicle."

That gave Marcus a feeling of satisfaction, knowing their only escape had been cut off. *Thank you, rangers.*

He stopped the truck and got out, spotting a figure hiding in the shadows of the concession building.

"That's far enough," Dillon stated as Marcus walked around the front of the SUV.

The rangers' voices in his ear responded back and forth that they could hear Dillon talking, thanks to Marcus's mike, but not one of them could see him. But Marcus could. He had a perfect line of sight to the man. Dillon was still dressed in his shiny loafers and slacks. He still looked to Marcus like a slicked-out used-car salesman on the lookout for his next prey.

One thing he noticed that caught his eye was that Dillon appeared to be unarmed. Marcus had yet to pull his gun, but he had it on him, ready to use, the weight and feel of it as familiar as his own arm.

"Where's Bethany?" he demanded.

Dillon flashed him a grin. "She's inside. Come on. I'll take you to her."

Marcus pulled his weapon to drive his own point home. "Yes, you will."

"Now, now, Marcus. There's no need for that. I'll

gladly take you to see your girl. I want to give you both a chance to say goodbye to one another."

He didn't like the sound of that. "Goodbye?"

"That's right. You're coming with me and the tale of the man who was raised from the dead will fade into obscurity. You'll either become a ghost tale, or the rumored story of a soldier who betrayed his country and was never heard from again."

"And what about Bethany?"

"She will be disgraced among the Agency when it's discovered that the Marcus Allen she found alive didn't really exist. She'll quietly retire and disappear from the government's radar."

It was the same scenario he'd given him in the barn. Now, why didn't Marcus believe it?

"I want to know she's safe before I come with you. Let her go now. She can take my truck and disappear."

"No. That's not happening."

Marcus pointed his gun at Dillon. "Then I'm not coming with you. We're going inside to get Bethany and we're both leaving here."

Dillon flashed him a grin again, this one smug and knowing. "That's not going to happen, either."

A shot rang out. Marcus couldn't tell from what direction it came, but a moment later it dug into the skin on his hand, jamming through bone and flesh and zipping out the other side. Searing pain pulsed through him, causing him to drop his gun and grab his hand, which was oozing blood.

Dillon howled with laughter. "Look at that. He made

the shot. It might be the only accurate one he makes today, but he did it."

In Marcus's ear, the rangers were shouting out to one another, trying to identify where the shot had originated. "I have no visual! No visual!" came their frantic yells.

"Draw him out," Matt yelled.

Shots began to ring out from all around Marcus, trying to pull the sniper into firing again and giving up his location.

Marcus fell to his knees, mostly trying to avoid the gunfire but also because the pain shooting through him was devastating. He used his teeth to tear off a piece of his shirt and wrapped it around his hand to stop the bleeding. He didn't think they would draw out the sniper. If he hadn't been hiding in the place the others had identified as the best proximity to shoot from, then he'd found another, even better, place to perch.

The voices in Marcus's ear and the sounds of gunfire around him made his head spin. Flashes of memory began flooding back to him. Another situation where he was trapped, rangers were yelling in his earpiece and shots were ringing out.

He tried to push the memories away and hold on to the reality of the moment. He couldn't get lost in them, not now.

Suddenly the images came to life and someone grabbed him. Dillon had managed to sneak up on him, knock him over the head and grab hold of his jacket. He dragged him to the other side of the SUV. His actions were so sudden and so unexpected that Marcus didn't even have time to protest or to fight back.

"I've got you now." Dillon dragged him toward the building as the sound of confusion and chaos played out in his earpiece.

"Ambush!" someone yelled. "It's a trap!" But Marcus couldn't be certain if he was hearing the shouts now through his earpiece or in the flashbacks that were flooding back to him.

Just then an explosion rocked the area that sent both him and Dillon reeling toward the underpinning of the concession building. Dillon swore and clicked on a mike in his ear. "What was that?" he demanded.

Marcus heard a voice respond, "Just a few RPGs."

Rocket powered grenades. The rangers hadn't been prepared for RPGs. He grimaced, realizing he had led them into an ambush again.

The memories kept coming, pouring back into his mind like a waterfall of horror and angst. He remembered scanning an area and seeing a familiar face lurking in the shadows. "You...you were there," Marcus rasped. "The night my team was ambushed."

Dillon huffed. "Of course I was there."

Another image flashed through his mind. An image of another man, a familiar face he couldn't quite see but he knew the uniform and the gear. Levi? Was it Levi he'd seen talking with Dillon that terrible night?

Dillon reached down and ripped out the earpiece and mike from Marcus's gear. The gunfire and sounds of explosions and yelling continued, proof that this was all happening in real time. Dillon yanked him to his feet and down a hallway. He opened a door and shoved him. Marcus tumbled inside, hitting a wall and sliding to the ground.

His vision was bleary but he saw Dillon grin just before he slammed the door closed. Then a face hovered over his. He jerked away, startled that he wasn't alone and uncertain where he was or who was with him.

"Marcus, are you hurt?"

He knew her voice the moment she spoke and suddenly her touch soothed him instead of startled him. Releasing a ragged breath, he saw an outline standing over him but he couldn't make out her face. He was fading fast, but he longed for one more look at her. He tried to reach for her face, but his hand refused to move.

"Beth," he managed to whisper and she eagerly responded.

"It's me. I'm here."

Then the last thing he knew was the feel of her lips on his as he faded away into darkness.

TEN

Marcus slumped against her and Bethany felt fear rattle through her. She checked his breathing. It was steady and his heart was beating strongly. That relieved her, but she could see that his hand was bleeding through the makeshift bandage wrapped around it. And he hadn't seemed to see her or even been able to stand when Dillon had shoved him inside.

She checked him for other wounds and found no other bleeding except for his hand. But when she felt his head, a large knot was already forming. Dillon must have hit him hard and unexpectedly. She took comfort in the fact that he would likely awaken soon.

She just hoped it was soon enough. The gunfire and explosions outside were deafening even from inside the concrete room where Dillon was keeping them. She thought it must have once been a freezer for the concession stand because of the shelves, the steel door and the lack of windows. What was happening out there? Were they in a war zone?

Marcus began to stir and she ran back to him on the floor, relief flowing through her.

He groaned and his eyes fluttered. "What happened?"

"I think someone hit you on the head. You've been unconscious for several minutes."

He grunted then tried to pull himself up. "Dillon." He spewed out the name with such animosity.

"Yes, I can't believe I ever trusted him."

He reached out and touched her face, his eyes brimming with elation before he pulled her into his arms. "I thought I'd lost you," he whispered.

She melted into his embrace. There was so much she wanted to say to him, to tell him that she knew he wasn't a traitor and apologize to him for ever believing he was. "I was afraid, too."

He framed her face with his hands. "Are you hurt?"

"No, I'm fine." Another blast shook the room. "For now."

He took her hand and squeezed it. "Don't worry. We'll get out of here. The rangers won't let anything happen to us."

"How can we trust them? Levi is working with Dillon and he's one of them, Marcus."

"So am I," he reminded her. "I can't explain it, but I trust them. Levi may be working with Dillon, but I guarantee the rest of the team didn't know it. They're on the lookout for him. They'll do the right thing."

"We have to get out of here."

"We will."

He started moving along the walls, looking for a

weakness. She had already done so earlier but she didn't mention it. She started again. There had to be some way out of this room.

An explosion detonated and the aftershock knocked Bethany to the ground. It was loud and close, and made the ground shake. Marcus hit the floor, too, but she saw more than shock on his face. Fear flashed across his eyes and he crawled to the corner, holding his head and giving a low, guttural groan.

She scuttled over to him. "What is it? What's wrong?"

His fingers dug into his head and he groaned again. "The images. I can't stop them. I…can't…"

She understood. Memories were flooding him. Memories of the night of the ambush, the attack against him and his team. The current battle must have brought them all back. He was paralyzed by them, unable to separate the real battle from the one occurring in his mind.

She gave a beleaguered sigh. What a time for him to regain his memories.

Bethany heard the lock on the door slide. She ran to the wall and braced herself. Marcus was helpless against Dillon and Levi like this. It was up to her to fight for them both.

The door opened and Dillon stepped inside, spotting Marcus huddled in the corner.

From behind the door, Bethany lunged for him before he turned and spotted her. She jumped, kicked the back of his knees, causing him to lose his balance, then she grabbed him around the neck and throat punched him.

Dillon's knees buckled and he went down but Bethany didn't let go. He'd taught her this move and probably never thought she would use it against him. The irony didn't escape her. She didn't release her grip as he struggled to grab her to no avail. Finally his hands went limp and he fell. But she also knew from his training that he wouldn't be out for very long. They had to get out of there now before Dillon regained his composure. She also checked him for a gun but found nothing but a Taser. It would have to do.

She grabbed Marcus's arm and he jerked at her touch.

"It's me," she said softly. "It's Bethany. We have to get out of here now."

He nodded, seeming to understand, and she helped him to his feet. She placed his arm over her shoulder and helped him out, past Dillon, who was still lying on the floor trying to catch his breath. But that didn't keep him from grabbing out for her. She turned and kicked him, knocking him back again and stuffing the urge to keep kicking him until he was unable to come for them again.

As she headed for the door, another explosion rocked the ground. Bethany stumbled and Marcus flinched at each round of gunfire. What was going on out there?

Dillon grabbed for her again and this time connected with her ankle, pulling it and yanking her off her feet. She hit the concrete and the Taser flew from her hand. Marcus fell, too.

Bethany spun around as Dillon lunged for her. She tried to kick him and grab for the Taser but he was faster getting to his feet. He scooped up the Taser and used it on her, sending unknown volts of electricity shooting through her. Bethany screamed then slumped and Dillon caught her. She'd completely lost control of her body with the pain ripping through her from the electrocution. He dragged her back into the freezer and left her lying on the floor, unable to move except for the jerks of her muscles, fighting to remain conscious. As he walked to the door, he spoke to her. "Don't try that again, Bethany. You can't defeat me."

Tears slid down her face as she fought to regain her motion. Was he right? Had he truly won?

And where was the God that Marcus believed so much in? Why wasn't He helping them?

Dillon turned from the door and Marcus kicked his legs out from under him. He'd made a huge mistake in assuming Marcus was too far out of it to know what was happening. Bethany's cries had helped him push through the flood of memories and grab hold of the here and now.

Dillon went down. Marcus leaped to his feet, grabbed Dillon up and slammed his head against the concrete hard enough to knock him out. He went limp and Marcus searched his pockets and bag, finding a roll of duct tape. He used it to bind Dillon's hands. He also found his keys and opened the door.

Bethany lay still on the concrete floor, causing a moment of panic to surge through him. He rushed to her side and rolled her over. She was twitching from the Taser blast, but she was slowly regaining movement.

"Are you okay, honey?" he asked urgently. "Can you speak?"

She tried but only managed to nod. He picked her up and cradled her gently against him as he carried her down the hall. They needed to find a way out of there and to contact the rangers. He passed a room where he saw a computer set up on a makeshift desk. It had to be Dillon's command center. His gun and radio were probably in there, too.

He walked in and carefully placed Bethany on the floor. "I'll be right back," he whispered and she managed to give him a small nod. He knew she was quickly regaining muscle control and would be fine in a few moments.

He moved to the computer and checked the screen. Several boxes appeared to have different camera angles covering the entire area. Dillon had this drive-in wired with cameras. Marcus could see several of the rangers gathered behind a concrete barrier from an overhead angle and another camera showed Levi loading up another RPG.

Marcus had to warn them. He glanced around and saw his gear in the corner. Pulling out his mike, he shoved in the earpiece and began to speak. "Rangers, this is Marcus. I have visual on Levi. Prepare for another RPG firing. He's in the trees on the east side of the camp. Repeat, he's on the east side in the trees."

"Roger that" came Matt's voice. A moment later the blast came, shaking the building.

Marcus ran to the front and saw that both vehicles were now in flames.

"Marcus, where are you? What's your status?"

"I'm inside the concession building. Dillon is down

and I have Bethany. He has cameras surrounding the place and streaming to a laptop in here. I'm on my way out there to help you."

"Negative," Garrett commanded. "Get Bethany and run. Get out of here. We'll take care of Levi."

The others agreed. He didn't like running, but he needed to get Bethany to safety. Of course, with their vehicles out of commission, they would have to make it to one of the ranger's vehicles. They were closest to the one Garrett and Blake had driven but they would have to go through the woods to reach it.

He knelt beside Bethany. "How are you feeling?"

"I'm better," she said, pushing to her feet. "I'm ready to go."

He slipped his gear on and grabbed his rifle.

"Marcus, look," she cried, pointing at the computer. "He's getting away."

He glanced at the screen and saw that Levi had abandoned his post and was disappearing into the woods. The gunfire outside continued, telling him his friends had no idea Levi was gone and probably wouldn't for several minutes. That was enough of a head start for him to get away and, if they didn't catch Levi in action, no one would ever be able to prove that he was involved. He could claim ignorance and, although the rangers might have their suspicions, they would always also have doubts.

He couldn't let him get away. Levi, like Dillon, had to pay for his crimes. He spoke into his microphone. "Levi is escaping into the woods. I'm going after him."

He stopped and looked at Bethany, suddenly realizing he couldn't leave her alone.

"Go," she told him. "Go get him. I'll be fine and I'll keep an eye on Dillon."

"Are you sure?" he asked, hesitant to leave her.

"I'm fine." She picked up the Taser that Dillon had used on her. "I'll be safe here."

He dragged Dillon into the room and set him in the corner. "Keep an eye on him," he told Bethany and she nodded, looking pleased at the task as she held the Taser in her hand.

"I almost hope he tries something."

He started to walk out then turned back. There was so much he wanted to say to her. He didn't want to wait to say it, but he had to. If he didn't go now, Levi would be gone for good. He touched her face and cut to the chase. "I remember," he told her. "I remember everything, and I promise you, Beth, my feelings for you were never faked."

Her face lit up but the pressure of the moment kept her from asking for more. She placed a quick kiss on his lips. "Go and come back to me soon."

He assured her he would be back and he meant it. Nothing would keep him away from her ever again.

Bethany glared at Dillon in the corner and he glared right back. Marcus had taped his hands and legs and mouth. She'd never seen him look so vulnerable. She owed him a world of hurt for all the grief he'd put her through. He'd shot Marcus, leaving him for dead, then pretended for years to care about her enough to follow her investigation. That alone, in her opinion, made him deserve a bullet to the head, but she didn't have the right to make those decisions. She would bring him in to the CIA and let them exact justice for his crimes. He had hurt more people than just her.

"You tried to break us," she said to him. "You tried to bring us down, but you couldn't." She couldn't help the smug tone of her voice. He deserved much worse. "Did you hear what he just said to me before he left? He said he remembers everything."

Dillon's eyes widened and he looked as if he wanted to lunge for her.

"He remembers, which means he knows what you were up to that night and he'll tell everyone. I'll be there to back him up. You've lost, Dillon."

She turned back toward the computer and looked at the images of the devastated drive-in. The gunfire had settled down since Marcus's report that Levi had escaped into the woods.

She set the stun gun on the desk and shook her head at all the violence Dillon's actions had caused. It infuriated her to know that one person could affect other people's lives in such a negative manner. It angered her, but it also annoyed her to know that God allowed such things. Marcus believed in Him and trusted Him, but, to Bethany, this was just one more thing that He could have prevented.

They'd already lost so much time together and she didn't want to spend another moment away from him. But was it likely that too much had happened between them to make a relationship possible? She didn't know, but she wanted them to have time together to figure out if they could make it work. But that meant she had to stop waiting and watching for the other shoe to drop. She sighed, wishing she didn't have such a negative opinion of everyone.

Would she ever feel like God was on her side again?

Something on the computer screen caught her attention, but it wasn't an image from the camera. It was a reflection in the screen of someone coming up behind her. She spun around and saw Dillon, now free of his binds, lunging at her, a knife in his hand. She kicked at him but he flew at her and knocked her to the floor. The Taser was still on the desk and she scolded herself for ever dropping her guard and putting it down. But how and where had Dillon gotten hold of a knife?

His pack was on the floor near where Marcus had placed him. She realized he must have gotten to it, grabbed the knife and cut himself free. She should have moved it just in case and she certainly should have never turned her back on him, tied up or not. She'd underestimated this man again, but it would be the last time she made that mistake.

He grabbed her and pulled her to her feet. "Sit down," he demanded.

She sat back in the chair as he scooped up the duct tape and wound it over her hands.

Once she was secure, he hit a button on the laptop and spoke. "Levi, where are you? What's your status?"

Levi's voice filtered through the speaker. "I'm in the woods. I'm safe but they're hunting me."

"Lose them and meet me at the rendezvous point. I've got the girl. That's all the leverage we need."

"Copy that."

He clicked off, closed the laptop then turned to her. "We're leaving now." Then he slapped her face hard. Pain radiated through her cheek and she nearly toppled over in the chair. When she glanced back up at him, he sneered.

"Who's the loser now, Bethany?"

Marcus ran through the woods, pushing away branches and scrubs, his only focus on finding Levi and bringing him in. The rogue agent had claimed to be in New Orleans when Colton had phoned him. Capturing him now and bringing him down was the only way to prove to everyone that he'd been lying about everything and had in fact been working with Dillon.

Marcus could leave no doubts if he ever wanted his life back. Now that he remembered everything that had happened that night in Afghanistan, he knew he had nothing to be ashamed of except for failing to take down both traitors that night he'd seen them together. It had seemed suspicious to him that Dillon had even been on-site. CIA personnel generally remained on the base for the duration of the mission.

"I've made arrangements to take down Akif," he'd heard Dillon say. "Everyone will think he's the one to blame."

"And the target is already off-site?" Levi had asked him.

"Yes, I informed his men about the pending operation and they moved him three hours ago. I made certain it was done during a time the drones wouldn't capture it on video."

Marcus remembered the anger that had whipped through him and he felt it again. It sickened him to realize that a member of his team and a CIA agent were talking so callously about walking American soldiers into an ambush. Now he knew he'd acted rashly in confronting them instead of relaying the information immediately back to his commanding officer.

Marcus spotted movement in the brush, pulling him back to the present day. He stopped, kneeling as he scanned the horizon, until he saw a figure running toward him.

He clicked on his mike. "I have eyes on the target. He's in the woods behind the concession building."

"On our way," he heard a multitude of voices proclaim.

He dropped his gun and took a place behind a tree. He didn't want the guy dead and he had the element of surprise on his side.

Marcus sprang forward and clotheslined him as Levi passed. He sent him falling backward and Levi groaned in pain as Marcus lunged at him, grabbing him by the jacket and pulling him to his feet. If it had been possible, he was certain steam would have been coming from his ears, his face felt so flush with anger.

"You betrayed us," Marcus snapped, more anger than he'd thought possible pouring out of him as he smashed his fist into Levi's face. He went down again but this time came back up fighting, blood oozing from a cut on his lip.

"I don't answer to you," he stated, not hesitating before tackling Marcus. The two men struggled on the ground and fought hand-to-hand, each throwing punches and blocking. They seemed evenly matched but Marcus's injured hand—the hand Levi had shot—put him at a distinct disadvantage and Levi took full advantage by grabbing it until Marcus screamed in pain.

He pushed through the pain and headbutted him, sending them both off balance and hitting the dirt. Instead of crawling to his feet and continuing the fight, Levi grabbed for the rifle that had flown from his hand when Marcus attacked. He grabbed it then spun at Marcus, who remained unarmed, his own gun still by the tree.

"Get up," Levi demanded.

Marcus glanced up at him then slowly crawled to his feet, defeated. "You betrayed us," Marcus said. "How could you do that? You betrayed us all."

"You don't know the meaning of the word *betrayal*," Levi shot back. "You all betrayed me."

"How did we betray you? You and Dillon are the ones who sent our entire squad to their deaths."

"Our government betrayed us, Marcus. They're the ones who sent us into dangerous situations with poor intelligence and inadequate weaponry. They're the enemy and you continue to fight for them even after they left you for dead."

He had heard this spiel before and imagined those were Dillon's words coming from Levi's mouth. Levi had only been a foot soldier recruited by Dillon and Marcus knew there must have been some vulnerability in Levi that he'd been able to expose. It saddened him to think someone he'd once considered a friend could have been so easily manipulated. But Levi had made a choice and he'd crossed a line from which he could never return. He was responsible for men's deaths and God was the only judge who could ever redeem him.

Levi touched his earpiece. "I have Marcus."

Marcus nearly smiled, knowing that Levi was speaking to no one on the other end of that mike. Dillon Montgomery was out of action. He'd made certain of it.

Levi appeared to be listening to someone then he clicked the mike and said, "Copy that."

Marcus's gut clenched. It wasn't possible he was talking to Dillon. Was there someone else they didn't know about in the mix?

"Who was that?" he asked. "Who were you talking to just now? Not Dillon. It couldn't be Dillon."

Levi gave him a chilling smile then removed his earpiece. "Repeat command," he stated. The voice that came through nearly sent Marcus to his knees.

"I said kill him" came Dillon's voice loud and clear. "Kill him now and let's get out of here. I have the girl. She's all the leverage I need to make it out of here alive. They won't dare do anything as long as she's my hostage."

Marcus felt his words like a punch to his gut. Dillon had escaped and had Bethany at his mercy. He wanted to kick himself for leaving her. He should have been with her. He should have known how dangerous a man Dillon Montgomery was.

"On your knees now," Levi said, aiming the gun at him.

Marcus dropped to his knees, knowing he had no other choice but also wondering what would happen to Bethany once he was gone.

Levi stood behind him.

He felt the barrel of the gun press against his head and knew his time was limited.

Lord, please take care of her. Please make a way out of this for her. I love her so much.

Marcus heard the safety of the gun release. This might be the end for him, but he was thankful that at least Bethany knew his feelings for her had been real. He kicked himself now for not saying he loved her. He hoped she wouldn't doubt his affection like she had for the past two years.

He closed his eyes and prayed. He wasn't ready to die. He'd just recovered his name, his reputation and his family. But most of all, he'd found Bethany again. He wasn't ready to let her go. But he'd trusted in God throughout this process and he couldn't stop now. His journey might have ended, but hers hopefully would continue.

Help her out of this, Lord. Please, keep her safe.

His only thought as the gun went off was of Bethany and how much he loved her.

She jerked when a shot rang out over the radio and a cry escaped her lips. Hot tears flooded her eyes and an overwhelming grief paralyzed her at the horrible real-ization that Marcus was dead.

She'd spent so long questioning him…so much time being angry with him over something that wasn't even his fault. Anger rushed through her. It wasn't fair! She'd joined the CIA because she wanted to make this world a better place. Her eyes were open now. Life wasn't easy and it wasn't fair.

Marcus would tell her to pray but she didn't know if she could. All that anger and hurt and betrayal she'd felt the first time she'd thought she'd lost him returned. She wanted to blame God but this time her anger was di-rected at a man and he was standing in front of her now.

She wouldn't allow him to get away with this. She didn't know how, but she would make it out of this situ-ation and somehow she would find a way to make him pay for what he'd done.

Dillon clicked on the mike. "Levi, respond. Is it done? Is he dead?"

There was no immediate response, which gave Beth-any a sliver of hope, but it was short-lived. A few mo-ments later the response came over the headset. "He's dead."

Sorrow burst through her at those two little words and Bethany knew at that moment that she couldn't go through this alone. She needed help but had no clue where to turn. She couldn't go through another two years of suffering like she'd done before. The anger and bitterness had eaten her up inside. And that was no way to live. She wanted a life and she wanted one day to be happy again.

Suddenly she realized she was looking at this all wrong. How many people got to spend time with someone they loved after they'd thought they'd died? She'd had that privilege, had gotten the answers she'd sought and had shared a few more precious moments with him. How could she be angry with a God that would give her such a gift?

Lord, I need You.

Her soul made the cry. She remembered the way Marcus described feeling someone higher than himself with him. She needed that assurance that she wasn't alone in the world and she needed the healing He could offer her.

Dillon slammed his laptop shut and grabbed her arm. "We're leaving."

She wiped away tears and tried to focus on the moment. First, she had to escape. She had no doubts that Dillon would not keep her alive long now that Marcus was dead. He had no use for her anymore except as a hostage to threaten if the rangers caught up with him. Once he was safely away, he would kill her for sure. She should have felt alone, but she didn't anymore. Marcus had told her to pray and she was ready. She didn't know if it would do any good. She was certain God could fix this all, but she knew He didn't always intervene. He might let this happen. She closed her eyes and prayed. She needed Him to act.

Finally she understood the truth of what Marcus had been telling her. Even if He didn't intervene to change her situation, God would see her through it. He would guide her on this new journey.

Dillon yanked her out the chair and through the dark hallway. Bethany spotted an unlit exit sign and knew they were heading that way. Did he have a car waiting? All of theirs had been destroyed. And what about the other rangers? She realized they were still out there. All hope wasn't lost. She just needed to keep her eyes open to possibilities to either overpower Dillon or to escape him.

He burst through the doors and into the back woods, but as he ran, his grip on her loosened. This was her one and only chance at escape. Could she succeed? Taking a deep, bracing breath, she pulled away from him and turned and ran the other way into the woods.

Dillon bellowed after her. "Stop! Get back here or I'll shoot."

She didn't stop. This was her only chance to make it out alive.

He fired several shots. She still didn't stop. It wasn't the first time she'd come under fire and she knew continuing to run was her best chance for survival. The branches kept smacking against her face, cutting into her skin, but it was a small price compared to what Dillon would do to her if he caught her.

Father, help me!

She heard movement in the woods and knew Dillon was chasing her. But where were the rangers? Reaching them was her only hope. She needed them on her side if she had any hope of making it out of this alive. She needed to head back toward them. It was a risk but one she had to take.

She stumbled over some exposed tree roots and fell,

landing hard on her shoulder and knee. She grimaced and got back up, but she wasn't quick enough. Dillon caught up with her, grabbed her around the waist and lifted her from the ground.

"Did you really think you could get away from me?" he rumbled in her ear. "You're not going anywhere."

She had made the decision she wasn't going down without a fight and she'd meant it. She kicked and struggled, trying to break his hold, to no avail. He overpowered her.

Suddenly several shots rang out, hitting the trees surrounding them.

Dillon ducked, grabbed her around the neck and pressed the knife in his hand to her throat as a group of men in survival gear appeared from the brush, each with a rifle trained on them.

"That was a warning shot," a voice told him. "Next time, we won't miss."

She recognized his voice right away. Marcus! He was alive!

The men cleared a path and Marcus stepped forward, dragging a bound and disarmed Levi behind him. He shoved him to the ground in front of them for Dillon to see.

"It's over, Dillon. Let her go. You've lost."

Dillon dug the blade into her skin and she cried out in pain, certain he'd broken skin. It would take only a slip of his hand to slit her throat. He started backing up. "I'm getting out of here and Bethany is my ticket to escape. Don't think I won't kill her."

"You won't," Marcus said. "You need her."

Her heart was racing as she realized she hadn't lost Marcus, and she wasn't going to, either, not this way. Knowing she had to get away from Dillon so the rangers could take him out, she jabbed her elbow as hard as she could into his stomach. He groaned and doubled over, but not before digging the blade deep into her throat. They went down together and she heard the sweet sound of gunfire end the standoff.

Marcus ran to her as the uncontrollable pain shook her. He pressed his hand at her throat and she knew it was bad from the frantic look on his face. He fell to the ground and pulled her into his lap. She noticed his breathing was heavy and sweat broke out on his forehead.

"Don't you leave me," he pleaded, his face going pale.

Another figure hovered over her and she recognized it was Matt. "Keep pressure on her wound," he told Marcus, then yelled at someone else. "Go get the truck. We have to get her to a hospital now."

She was aware of Marcus ripping pieces of his jacket and pressing it against her neck.

Breathing became difficult and she suddenly felt weak. She was thankful she was already in his arms. This was where he wanted to be. It was the only place she wanted to be, as well.

"Come on, Beth," Marcus said, shaking her gently and rousing her. She hadn't realized she was drifting off. "Don't you do this to me. You spent all that time and energy looking for me. Don't you leave me now."

It took effort, but she managed to lift her hand and

touch his face. He covered her hand with his own and she realized his face was wet with tears.

"I love you," she whispered, choking over the words and not even sure she got them out.

She must have because he leaned down and kissed her forehead. "I love you," he whispered in her ear.

She clung to his words as she slipped away.

Lord, please don't let me lose her.

Marcus had spent most of the past two days—ever since Dillon Montgomery had slit her throat like the animal he was—on his knees, praying for Bethany's healing and recovery. She'd lost a lot of blood before they'd made it to the hospital and an infection had set in after surgery, causing concern by her doctors. Finally she'd turned a curve and seemed to be resting comfortably, but the antibiotics and pain medication they were pumping into her kept her groggy and subdued and he hated seeing her this way.

He camped out in her hospital room, taking up residence in the recliner at her bedside and daring anyone to try to move him. The only one who had was Rick Eaves. Bethany's CIA supervisor had tried to get him to return to Langley for questioning at the same time the Marshals had picked up and transported Dillon and Levi for the trip.

The rangers had shot Dillon, but hadn't killed him. He'd been treated and released to the Marshal's custody. Marcus had refused to leave, reminding Rick that he'd instructed Bethany to bring him in and that's what would happen.

Her hospital door opened and Marcus looked up to see Colton. He got up and greeted him, shaking his hand heartily.

"How is she doing?" Colton asked, motioning toward the bed.

"She's doing good," Marcus assured him. "She's going to pull through."

Colton, however, looked rough, as if sleep had evaded him, as well, the past two days. "How are you?"

He nodded, an instinctive response, Marcus decided. "I'm getting there. I won't lie to you. It was a shock for us all finding out what Levi had been doing all this time. That CIA guy told me that all those surgeries he claimed to have, they've discovered that they coincided with the dates Bethany was out searching for you. I guess Dillon was covering for him, forging his records somehow." He grimaced. "He was badly hurt in the ambush, just not as seriously as he led us all to believe. He hasn't needed any additional surgeries. I always thought it was odd that he didn't want any of us with him at the hospital. I just thought it was vanity, that he didn't want us to see him weak like that."

Marcus saw the sorrow in his friend's face and couldn't help feeling responsible. "I'm sorry for the role I played in all this."

Colton waved him away. "It wasn't your fault, Marcus. One thing I've learned recently is that God works things out in ways we don't always understand."

Marcus glanced at Bethany and knew that was true. They'd spent nearly two years apart and he was still struggling to wrap his brain around why that had been necessary.

Colton pulled a slip of paper from his pocket. "I can't stay, but I wanted to give you this. I wrote all our phone numbers and addresses down for you. In case you need anything, you'll know who to call. And once Bethany is up and better, we'd like you both to come back to the ranch for a get-together. The fellas will all bring their wives and you can get to know the whole crew again."

Marcus nodded, liking that idea. New old friends.

He shook Colton's hand and wished him well. He and the others had really come through for them and he owed them a deep gratitude. If not for them, he and Bethany would both likely be dead.

He glanced at her, unmoving and still, and the pain shook him again—the terror he'd felt at the thought of losing her. It had nearly done him in when he'd seen Dillon dig that knife into her throat. Marcus had truly believed that was the end for them.

He slipped back into the recliner, picked up his Bible and got back to his prayers, thankful that God seemed to have other plans for them.

Bethany opened her eyes. Her gaze roamed over the room, noticing the hanging curtain, the TV mounted on the wall and a light coming from the bathroom. She turned to glance at it and saw Marcus sitting in a chair by the bed. He was hunched over and whispering a prayer.

She tried to speak to him, to get his attention, but all she managed to do was to make a gurgling sound and even that hurt her throat. But it was enough. He heard her and glanced up, a smile breaking across his face as he moved closer to her side and reached for her hand.

"Welcome back," he said, squeezing her hand.

"What happened?" she asked, trying again to speak. This time it came out but as a squeak instead of the determined tone she'd meant to portray.

"You're safe," he told her. "Dillon cut your throat. Do you remember that?"

She tried to nod then realized that hurt just as much. "Hard to forget." She would always remember the feeling of that knife slicing into her. She'd tried to be brave and tried to make her escape.

"He can't hurt you anymore," Marcus reassured her. "He and Levi have both been turned over to the authorities. Your supervisor, Rick, sent the Marshals to take them back to Langley. He also called to congratulate you on a job well done and to tell you they followed up on Bill Donahue checking out your phone records and determined it was Dillon using his identification number. It's one more charge to add to his growing list of crimes."

She was glad to hear that both Dillon and Levi had been exposed and were no longer a threat to anyone.

"He wanted me to come in, too, but I told him I would only allow you to bring me in." He gave her a smile then kissed her hand. The truth was he wasn't going anywhere until he knew Bethany was on her way to recovery. "I guess he could tell I was serious because he backed down and gave the okay for me to stay here with you."

She smiled then grimaced as she moved. "It still hurts."

"You were crying out in your sleep a while ago so I buzzed the nurse. She should be bringing you more pain medicine soon."

"How long have I been here?"

"Two days."

Two days! She didn't remember anything since being in the woods and discovering Marcus was still alive. Suddenly the moment she'd heard Levi proclaim he was dead came rushing back.

"What happened?" She wanted to know. "I thought—" She choked over the words but it had nothing to do with her injuries. "I thought you were dead. I heard Levi say that you were dead."

His face flushed with embarrassment. "I know, I know. I'm sorry. Levi did tackle me in the woods. I thought he was going to kill me. I was terrified because I thought I would never get to see you again."

"What happened?" she repeated.

"The rangers showed up. They shot him before he shot me. Seeing him that way with a gun to my head, well, it wasn't difficult for them to believe what I'd told them about him working with Dillon. Just as I thought, he tried to talk his way out of it, but they've all separately told me they don't believe him. But we still needed to get you out before Dillon harmed you, so Josh disguised his voice and made the call saying he'd shot me. I had no idea you would hear that message. I can't image how that must have felt."

"It devastated me, Marcus. I thought I'd lost you again."

"I know. I'm sorry. When I saw him cut you, Bethany, I nearly died myself. I was so afraid I was going to lose you. I don't think I've had a moment of peace about that until just now when you awoke. When I think how you must have felt for two years believing I was dead..." He shook his head and his voice cracked. "I'm so sorry I ever put you through that. I made you a promise that I would come back and I didn't keep it."

She looked at him. "You said you remembered everything. Didn't you tell me that?"

"Yes, I do. I remember it all. I remember you and me and the most amazing two weeks of my life." His eyes grew serious. "I also remember that I asked you a question that night before I left for the ambush. Do you remember that?"

Tears filled her eyes and she nodded. She knew exactly what question he was referring to.

"I asked you to marry me, Bethany."

Tears streamed down her face. "And I said no because it was too fast."

He chuckled ruefully. "Yes, you did tell me no."

"What you don't know, Marcus, what I never got an opportunity to tell you, was that I changed my mind. The moment that truck rolled away, I knew I never wanted to be separated from you. I know it was fast and it made no sense, but it was real. I think that's why it hit me so hard when I thought you'd lied about loving me." She reached out, caressed his face and drew in a choked breath. "But it was true. Wasn't it? Everything you told me was true."

"Well, not everything."

She gave him a quizzical look. What did he mean? Had he lied to her about his feelings, after all?

"When you rejected my proposal, I told you I understood and that I was okay with waiting." He laughed. "That was such a lie."

She laughed, too, at the absurdity of the moment. Why hadn't she just followed her heart right then and there?

"I was devastated. I went into that mission rocked and ready for a fight. I was stupid and I was reckless. I should have called my commander the moment I heard Dillon and Levi talking, but instead I tried to confront them. We all know how that worked out."

But it had worked out for them in the end. Bethany squeezed his hand then closed her eyes and said a silent prayer. God, it seemed, had been on her side, after all.

She stroked his face. "I love you, Marcus Allen."

He took in a sharp breath then smiled and leaned into her touch. "I love you, too, Bethany Bryant, and I'm never letting you go again."

He kissed her and she took comfort in his promise. It was one she would make sure he kept.

EPILOGUE

Bethany stood at attention as the director of the CIA pinned a medal to her chest and handed her a plaque in recognition of her achievement in bringing down Dillon and other traitorous agents. It held only her name and no specifics of the case, but it meant a lot to have the Agency approve her involvement. Dillon had hoped to disgrace her and cause her to slink away in embarrassment. Now he was the one sitting in a jail cell and facing the humiliation of his crimes.

As the director finished and the crowd clapped, she glanced around at the small group that had been allowed to attend the ceremony. She smiled when she spotted Marcus, standing and clapping for her. When the ceremony ended, she headed for him but was stopped before she reached him by well-wishers who wanted to congratulate her. Rick was one of them.

"You did it, Bethany. You actually did it. I'm very proud of you."

"Thank you, Rick."

"You really proved yourself with all this, Bethany.

You took action when you had to. I hope this means you've overcome your reluctance with field work. You always were one of my best agents. We need you out there."

She glanced at Marcus, uncertain what her future held. All she knew was that she wanted it to be with him. But how would he feel about her going back into action? "Can I let you know?" she asked.

Rick followed her gaze to where Marcus stood then turned back to her and nodded. "Of course. The job is yours if you want it."

She headed for Marcus and wished for nothing more at the moment than to fall into his arms, but she knew it wouldn't be appropriate since she was surrounded by her coworkers and government officials.

"You looked amazing up there," he told her gruffly. "I'm so proud of you."

"I couldn't have done it without you, Marcus." She laughed, realizing just how true that statement was.

She glanced at his hand still sporting a bandage. "How are you doing?"

"I'm okay. I've got several more days of debriefing, but my mom and Shannon are flying up for a few days so that'll be nice. I promised them no one would be shooting at them this time." He gave a little chuckle then shook his head "It's amazing the amount of paperwork it takes to come back to life. I've got meetings with lawyers, generals, accountants. The list goes on. Apparently, the government wants to capitalize on my apparent resurrection."

She glanced around the ceremony room. It seemed

odd that the army wanted to publicize the story while the CIA wanted to bury it. Were they even working for the same government?

"Rick just offered to put me back in the field."

"That's great news. You deserve it."

"I'm not sure I'm going to take it. I just don't know if that's the right course of action for me now." She hesitated before continuing. They'd both declared their love for one another during a moment of distress, but since their return to Virginia they hadn't discussed any future together. "How can I make a decision like that when I don't even know what my future holds?"

He gave her a look of understanding then looked away, his face reddening.

She nearly kicked herself. Why could she be so fearless in the field but act like a little girl when faced with matters of love? Was it possible he didn't see the same future for them together that she did?

"I want to be with you, Bethany, more than anything. Even though I know I don't deserve you."

She reached for his hand, rules of decorum forgotten. "You've been exonerated, Marcus. You've done nothing to be ashamed of. I'm the one who should be begging your forgiveness. I doubted you. I believed the worst about you. That you could lie and betray, but mostly that you would try to manipulate my heart for your own purpose. I should have never doubted you."

He smiled and put his hands on her face, tilting her chin up to stare into her eyes. "Honey, if you hadn't doubted me, would you have come looking for me?"

She gasped. She hadn't even thought of that. What

if she had never suspected Marcus of being a liar and a traitor? She imagined she would have gone about her life, allowing time to heal her grief over her lost love. Perhaps she even would have told herself she'd imagined how passionately she'd fallen for Marcus and down-played the truth about their love for one another. He was right, of course. Still, how could she have doubted him?

"In truth, we'd only known each other a short time. Two weeks is hardly enough time to get to know an-other person so completely."

"Maybe. After all, I don't even know what your fa-vorite color is."

He looked at her and smiled. "It's blue, of course, like the color of your eyes. They had me captivated from the first moment I saw them, from the first moment I saw you, Bethany."

She stroked his chin, loving the feel of his stubble against the softness of her hand then tears pooled in her eyes. "I don't understand why this happened. Why did God have to take you away from me for so long? Why did He have to put us through this?"

"I don't know the answer to that. But I think maybe He wants us to seek Him as hard and determinedly as you sought after me. I wouldn't be here if God hadn't been with me, watching over me, leading me back to my life." He smiled. "Back to you. If you'll have me."

Her heart soared. "I absolutely will. I love you so much, Marcus. I can't imagine my life without you."

"Then you don't have to. But you have to make me a promise. I want you to take that field job. It's what you love and you're good at your job."

"Okay. I'll tell Rick tomorrow. But what about you? What are your career plans now that you've gotten your life back?"

"Back to the rangers, I suppose. Technically, I never left the service." He stroked her face softly. "Do you think you could handle being married to someone with such a dangerous job?"

She smiled up at him and caught her breath. Had he just said he wanted to be with her forever? "I can if you can."

He leaned down and kissed her. "I can't promise you I'll always come home."

She leaned into him and smiled, feeling everything in her life finally settling into place. The best job, the best love and even a new relationship with the Lord. No matter what happened between them now, she would always trust in their love and trust that God was on their side.

"That's okay," she whispered. "I will always find you."

* * * * *

Dear Reader,

Fun fact: Marcus Allen was never supposed to be a hero. When I started my Rangers Under Fire series, this character wasn't even a blip on my radar. He didn't show up in the series until book four and even then it was only a paragraph or two about his being killed in the ambush and how his body was never recovered. He was a side note, a character meant to explore the depths of one of my other rangers...until he became so much more. Those few mentions captured the hearts and minds of my readers, my editor and even my mom. They all were hoping they would see Marcus Allen again at some point.

So Marcus began to grow in my imagination and eventually became everything I expected my final ranger to be. This character was the perfect hero to end the series and I couldn't be more pleased with how his story turned out. I hope you are, too.

Thank you for joining me and my Rangers Under Fire for this thrilling journey.

Blessings,
Virginia

COMING NEXT MONTH FROM
Love Inspired® Suspense

Available February 6, 2018

THREAD OF REVENGE
Coldwater Bay Intrigue • by Elizabeth Goddard

When marine biologist Sadie Strand returns home to find out who killed her friend, she's drugged and left on a sinking boat to die. But Coast Guard special agent Gage Sessions, an old friend, comes to her rescue—and refuses to leave her side when the attacks don't stop.

BABY ON THE RUN
The Baby Protectors • by Hope White

After witnessing the murder of her best friend, Jenna North flees with the woman's child. Now with someone after both her and the toddler, the only person she can trust is undercover FBI agent Matthew Weller.

PLAIN JEOPARDY
by Alison Stone

Back in her Amish hometown to recuperate from surgery, journalist Grace Miller follows leads on her mother's cold-case murder. But with someone dead set on stopping her from finding the truth, local cop Conner Gates must keep her safe.

CREDIBLE THREAT
by Heather Woodhaven

Someone wants Rebecca Linn—the granddaughter of a federal judge—dead, and it's Deputy US Marshal Kurt Brock's duty to uncover why. But with her life in his hands, can he resist falling for her...and make sure she survives?

MOUNTAIN REFUGE
by Sarah Varland

After narrowly escaping a murderous attack, Summer Dawson discovers she's the latest target of a serial killer. But her brother's friend, ex-cop Clay Hitchcock, is determined she won't become the killer's next victim—even if it means risking his own life.

HIGH-RISK INVESTIGATION
by Jane M. Choate

Reporter Scout McAdams won't let anything stop her from continuing the investigation that got her true-crime writer mother killed—even threats on her life. The criminals are determined to keep the truth hidden, though, and she can't turn down protection from former army ranger Nicco Santonni.

LISCNM0118

Get 2 Free Books,
Plus 2 Free Gifts —
just for trying the Reader Service!

"Jenna, it's me," Matthew said before entering the office.

He opened the door…

To the sight of Jenna wielding eight-inch scissors in her hand.

He suspected she'd be panicked, which was why he'd announced himself. He also knew she'd probably commit assault in order to protect the child.

"Let's go," he said, ignoring her terrified expression and the white-knuckled grip of the weapon.

She didn't move at first.

"We've gotta get out of here, and I mean yesterday." He motioned with his hands. "The baby okay?"

That seemed to redirect her trauma. She glanced at the child leaning against her shoulder. "Yes, he's fine."

"Good. Then let's go."

She started toward the door.

"I don't think you'll need the scissors."

She glanced at her hand.

"Unless you want to bring them, which is fine. We've gotta

make tracks here, Jenna."

"Right, of course." She dropped the scissors on the desk and followed Matt. "I saw you on the floor. That man with a gun, and then…" She glanced at him with questions in her eyes.

"I was able to neutralize him."

"So the security guard wasn't working with him?"

"No, ma'am. I flashed my ID and told him the woman and child who accompanied me to the hospital were being taken into protective custody."

They reached the exit and she hesitated.

"What?" he said.

"I won't let them take Eli away from me." She took a step backward. "I won't return him to his father."

"I know and I understand. Right now I need to get you and Eli safe. That's all I'm concerned with. I'm not sure I can trust my own people at this point. But you and me? We have to trust each other. What do I need to do to make you trust me, Jenna?"

"You won't take him back to his father?"

"No."

Matt had just made a promise, one that might require him to break the law. He didn't know what had compelled him to say it, but he had to get Jenna and the child out of here. He doubted the guy out front was alone.

She studied him with that assessing look of hers. "Fine I will try trusting you."

"You'll try?" he said, pushing open the door.

"I haven't had much success trusting people."

He guided her through the back lot, his eyes assessing, watching for signs of trouble. "Have a little faith."

Don't miss
BABY ON THE RUN by Hope White,
available February 2018 wherever
Love Inspired® Suspense books and ebooks are sold.

www.LoveInspired.com

Inspirational Romance to Warm Your Heart and Soul

Join our social communities to connect with other readers who share your love!

Sign up for the Love Inspired newsletter at **www.LoveInspired.com** to be the first to find out about upcoming titles, special promotions and exclusive content.

CONNECT WITH US AT:

Harlequin.com/Community

 Facebook.com/LoveInspiredBooks

 Twitter.com/LoveInspiredBks

LISOCIAL2017